THE VAMPIRE...IN MY DREAMS

VAMPIRE CHRONICLES
BOOK 1

TERRY SPEAR

FOREWORD

Synopsis

Proving a guy is a vampire for the glory it will bring seemed like a good idea to Marissa Lakeland. At the time. Until Dominic Vorchowski needs Marissa Lakeland's help to fight the vampire who made him the way he is. No problem. She's a witch. Witches can handle it. But vampires don't exist, and there's nothing in a witch's training that deals with a creature that doesn't exist. So using her wits, she'll manage, right? If the creature of the night doesn't get her first. As a centuries-old vamp, Lynetta doesn't lose ever, and she doesn't intend to now.

Yet, Marissa can't let the vamp have her way, not when Dominic's life depends on it. And so does her own.

To my daughter, Jennifer, who is my first reader on all of my young adult stories and encourages everything I do. I couldn't do it without her. Thanks, Jenn, for always being there for me, even when you're busy with schoolwork, at which time you give me a raised brow and incredulously say, "Don't tell me you want me to reread the whole changed manuscript, again?" But you always do. Thanks!
To her friend, Jaygen, who read the book also and loves vampires as much as we do!

1

M ARISSA

CHASING ONE of the undead was *not* my idea of a good time.

"Hold up, Kate!"

I ran to catch up to her in the heavily wooded neighborhood where we lived. She would be the death of both of us if the guy we stalked really was a vampire.

Ornate wrought iron streetlights cast a soft glow, coloring the mist a pale yellow, and an orange moon attempted to make its presence known, blurred behind the screen of light fog. Rustling eerily, fresh green leaves on the live oaks and ash lining the two-lane street danced in the breeze, casting shivering shadows, setting my nerves on edge. Crickets filled the night with their sing-song tune. Cool air clashed with the sun-warmed earth. Typical heart of Texas weather in early spring. The sweet fragrance of grape hyacinth teased the air, but something else drifted on the breeze, something manlier and spicier. Something that came from the direction we were headed.

Kate's flaxen hair flowed behind her like she was a golden goddess. Her makeup perfect, her midnight blue spandex running clothes fitting her curves, she looked like a star no matter where she was or what she was doing. Whereas I chugged way behind her in my light-colored blue jeans and blouse, hoping that the perspiration trickling between my breasts didn't begin to appear on the silk. The breeze tangled my long, blond hair, making me look like I'd been swept up by a tornado and spit back out. Everything about me paled in comparison to model-like Kate.

"Kate!" I implored, losing the race. Shin splints attacked my legs, and a stitch ran up my left side, each shooting pain into my out-of-shape body. I felt like I needed to be hospitalized...and soon.

Thicker fog gobbled Kate up, crickets elevated their raucous tune, and an owl hooted somewhere nearby.

A shimmer of white vapor blanketed the inky void ahead like an opaque barrier and I felt that if I penetrated it, I would be whisked into another world.

"Kate?" I no longer heard her size nine sneakers pounding the concrete sidewalk and my gut tightened with apprehension, but I tried to tell myself we were safe. That the guy we were chasing was not a vampire. That neither of us had anything to fear but what our own wild imaginations dug up.

Slowing my step, I attempted to catch my breath, the blood pounding in my ears. Adrenaline coursed through me like a river run amuck when a draft of cold air struck me from behind.

I couldn't turn around to look. A whiff of subtle spice whirled around me like an invisible cloak. Was Kate still chasing after the unseen vampire, while he now stalked me instead? *But they don't exist*, I hurriedly reminded myself.

Shoot. I hadn't even *wanted* to find out whether he was a vampire or not. Well, maybe I was a little curious, but not enough to get bitten. Kate was the adventurer of the two of us, and bullheaded. Ever since she'd spied the guy at the corner all-night hamburger joint, she'd insisted he was a vampire. The black clothes he wore, the darkly amused look. A Goth, I had explained. But she wasn't buying it. A vampire—that was what she insisted he was, and we were going to prove their existence, once and for all.

I itched to turn around and see if he stood behind me. I know, I know, curiosity killed the cat. But I had to look. I told myself nothing was there, but what my overwrought imagination told me stood there—a seriously magnificent guy, seventeen or eighteen years old in appearance, but hundreds of years old in reality, outfitted with a pair of razor-sharp, sabertooth tiger fangs. That's what I envisioned.

I turned and my jaw dropped. He was all there. All drop-dead gorgeous six feet of him. Darkly seductive, he wore ebony black jeans, matching sneakers, and a black T-shirt. I looked up at his face, hoping the fangs were still well-hidden and under control.

His deep brown eyes darkened to midnight and his lips curved up. I breathed a guarded sigh of relief to find no fangs extended. His dark brown hair showed off his square jaw and handsome angular features.

"Are you...are you...?" I wasn't normally a stutterer, but the realization I was alone in the dark with a possible vampire sent a rack of shudders through me, at the same time wreaking havoc with my tongue.

"Dominic Vorchowsky," he offered, and bowed his head slightly.

Definitely a vampiric action if I'd ever seen one. Suave, polite, enticing.

His voice had a strange melody, a strong, sensual attraction —just like I imagined vampires were supposed to have. His eyes gazed at mine with such intensity I wondered if he was attempting to draw me under his spell. He would woo me, then bite me and make me his forever. The notion should have made me ill, but the look in his hungry eyes lured me to drink every bit of him in. No one had showed that much interest in me, *ever*. For an instant, I was ready to bare my throat and let him take me.

"And you are Marissa Lakeland."

The way he said my name made it sound like his tongue rolled over each letter, every syllable, with undying affection. My heart skipped a beat. Vampires could control humans easily, so I'd read. I straightened my back. But I was a witch, and he should have no power over me. *So there.*

I folded my arms. "Are you a...?" Suddenly my gray matter focused on the words he'd spoken. "How do you know my name?"

He waved his hand at the night sky with a gallant gesture. "It's written in the stars."

"Right." Witches often used mumbo jumbo like that to confuse the general non-witch population, but he was no warlock. Or was he? "And why would my name be written in the stars?"

"We were destined to meet, you and I, on this very eve." He sounded so sincere, not at all teasing, though I didn't believe him for an instant.

"We make our own destiny," I said matter-of-factly, tilting my chin up slightly, like I always did when I knew I was right or at least wanted to assure another person I knew I was right.

He took a step forward and the action forced chill bumps to erupt all over my arms. Luckily, the long-sleeved, silky blouse I wore sufficiently hid the physical reaction I had to his presence.

I tilted my chin up even more, determined not to step away from him as much as I longed to do so. My witch's training was far from complete and an ancient vampire, if that was what he was, would be vastly more powerful than me, wouldn't he? At least from the fictionalized accounts I'd read, they were. Certainly, I had no desire to test my theory one way or the other.

Not that I was a coward or anything. But I never saw myself as being really stupid either. Except that I'd agreed to chase after sprinter Kate in the dead of the night trying to locate a vampire who now very likely stood before me.

My throat grew parched, both from running like a horse in a madcap race to the finish line, and from the sheer terror that threatened to undo me when I attempted to pose the question dangling from my dry tongue. Yet I still clung to the words, not sure I truly wanted to know the answer to the question that fought to be asked.

"Isn't it a little late for you to be out at night?" he asked, ruining my chance at questioning him first.

"Trying to get in shape," I fibbed. It wasn't an out-and-out lie. I had considered running to get in shape. But between playing video games, doing homework, reading for fun and doing chores that were not, I could never manage a formal P.T. schedule. I blurted out, "Are you a—"

He raised a brow, stopping my question in mid-sentence. "Would you truly like to know the answer to your question?" His words dipped low and sounded awfully ominous.

A gentle nudging tugged at my mind, but he couldn't read my thoughts. At least I didn't think so...or maybe it was powerfully wishful thinking. Still, I figured with my being a witch, if I chose not to allow him to read my mind, he couldn't. Yet, he seemed to know just what I was going to ask.

I hesitated. Was it a trick question? If he said he was a vampire, then would he have to kill me for revealing the truth?

Or was it that he was concerned I would be terrified when I knew the whole story?

Tamping down my normally cautious nature, I steeled my back, trying to make my five-foot-four height seem not so short. "Well, are you?"

He grinned. No fangs appeared. But then, maybe they had to extend, like when he smelled blood, or if he grew angry. As long as he was smiling, I figured it was a good sign. "Well?"

"You really don't want to know the answer to that question." Again, his voice held a menacing quality.

Sure I did. Didn't I? Cold seeped into the marrow of my bones, and I wasn't sure if I truly did want to know what he was.

Running footsteps sounded from the direction Kate had disappeared in, headed back in my direction. I turned and watched for her reappearance, glad to have backup. It sounded like she was running half her sprint-like speed now. How far had Kate gone before she realized the vampire no longer moved in front of her, or that I no longer followed behind?

"Marissa?" Kate called out anxiously.

"I'm here!" I remained standing next to my important catch —the Goth, or vampire, or whatever the guy was.

"What happened to you?" she called out from the fog.

I still couldn't make out her form, but the guy behind me gave a dark chuckle. Ignoring him, I hollered back, "I couldn't keep up with your long stride!"

"I lost him somewhere up ahead." Kate suddenly stepped out of the curtain of mist, her hair disheveled but still just as sexy. No unsightly perspiration marred her perfect skin, nor did she appear out of breath like I had been, gasping for air like a half-dead fish out of water. "I was sure I kept seeing his cape fluttering in the breeze just ahead of me. But when I realized you weren't behind me, I grew worried."

Cape? He wasn't wearing a cape. "Well, he's right here."

Proud of my accomplishment for once, I motioned to Dominic, standing behind me.

Kate looked around me. "Right."

I turned. Dominic was gone. Chill bumps freckled my skin again, and I took a deep breath, partly to calm my anxiety, and partly in exasperation that he would disappear and leave me behind to explain what had happened. "He was right here."

I looked back at Kate, but skepticism was written all over her face. She'd been chasing after him all along as far as she was concerned. No way did she want to think I had been speaking with him while she attempted to run down a phantom.

Kate folded her arms and quirked a sculpted blond brow. "All right. So was he one or not?"

She believed me? Well, I wasn't one to make up stories, good thing for me, so I guess that's the reason she didn't think I was doing so now. "He told me in so many words it wasn't a good idea to know the answer to that question."

Kate snorted, although the way she did it, she sounded classy. She was every guy's heartthrob. In fact, I couldn't understand why Dominic had left instead of engaging in a conversation with her. Her charming ways encouraged any guy to talk to her. Heck, if he had been leading us on a wild goose chase, why not visit with her in the cloak of fog up ahead, instead of coming back to see me?

"Right. So you didn't pin him down on an answer." Kate stalked back toward our street, but her voice definitely held a modicum of disbelief. I swore she muttered, "Like he was really there at all."

Now *that* ticked me off. She didn't believe me after all. I might not be as good at spells and concocting potions as she was, but I didn't make up tales and she knew it. It wasn't because I was Miss Perfect Goody Two-Shoes either, but the tips of my ears had a way of blushing when I fibbed, and everyone was aware of it.

"You don't believe me?" I tried to keep my voice even, and the venom out of it, but the poison coated my words anyway. It wasn't my idea to chase the...well, whatever he was, and it wasn't my fault I couldn't keep up with Kate. *And* it *definitely* wasn't my fault he targeted me instead of her. Was it that he figured I would be easier prey? Sure, Kate could sweet talk her way into or out of anything with a guy. Me? As of tonight, I just stuttered.

"I saw him ahead of me! Or at least his cape for a long time," Kate challenged with a hot backward glance at me while I tried to keep up.

The stitch in my side returned, and the shin splints hurt with every rushed step I took.

"They can just appear and disappear at random," I glibly replied as if I knew all about them. At least that's what the books of authority said on the subject of vampires. Though I didn't believe Kate was correct in thinking she'd been chasing the vampire all that long since he'd been with me for a while.

"I suppose you didn't do any of your tests on him either."

My heart sank. *No.* Just being in Dominic's mystifying presence had addled my brain, and I'd completely forgotten about the tests. But vampires were like the Loch Ness monster, Bigfoot, and the Abominable Snowman—unproven myths. Would our witch's tests really verify Dominic was a vampire?

Boy, had I blown it this time. I could have been the first witch to prove that vampires truly existed in our world. I would be instantly famous and maybe a warlock would look my way for once. Yeah, Joshua Cantaleaver—dark-haired, dark-eyed, lips of sin. If I were famous, he would want me. I would be the most popular girl in school. My teachers would look at me with respect and admiration. Even my parents would quit nagging me about my average grades. Inwardly, I smiled. *Dominic, you are going to make me famous.*

I shook my head at Kate, whose sharp green eyes studied me, waiting for a response to her question. "No, I didn't use any tests on him. I learned his name though."

Kate rolled her eyes.

"Dominic. Dominic Vor...something ending in a 'ski'."

"Did he have fangs?"

"Not that he extended. But he had a mouthful of perfectly straight teeth. Beautiful smile."

"You're hopeless. Here we had a chance to identify our first vampire, and you blew it."

At least she believed me now that I had spoken to him. However, somehow, I didn't think my chance meeting with Dominic was a one-time occurrence. In fact even now, the hair at the nape of my neck stood on end while I imagined he watched us from the dark. Waiting for what? To tell me the truth? To turn me into one of his own kind? To devour me alive upon our next meeting? Or was there some deeper meaning to our having met the way we did?

The wind whistled around my head, blowing my hair into my eyes. "*Marissa,*" it seemed to say. My blood chilled. Then I saw him, or what I perceived as him, a shadowy form half hidden by the spring green leaves of a towering maple, shivering in the cool breeze.

Kate had once again outdistanced me with her longer stride, and I ran to catch up. "Wait up!" I hadn't meant to sound so...scared.

I glanced back at the tree, but no sign of the shadow appeared now. Had he heard our entire conversation? Did he know we intended to prove he was a vampire?

My face heated. Why did he target me, instead of Kate with the golden hair? Tall and graceful, she was every guy's dream—

from the football jock to the rodeo dude. Me? Short and incon-spicuous. Did Dominic think that no one would notice if I suddenly just vanished from the face of the earth?

Kate glanced back at me. "I wonder why he came back to see you. Are you sure it was the same guy we saw at the burger place?"

Was she inferring I wasn't good enough? I tilted my chin up...all-knowing-like and in a most dramatic fashion replied, "We were destined to meet."

Kate stared at me, a disbelieving frown knitting her brows.

I shrugged. "So he said."

She shook her head. "Sounds like a guy line if ever I heard one." Her pace slowed though, and the tone of her voice sounded a bit worried.

I glanced behind me, the uneasy sensation of being stalked trickling through my bones. "Yeah, but from a regular guy or from a—"

"*Shhh,*" the wind whispered back.

2

DOMINIC

"I AM THE PRINCE OF DARKNESS," I said quietly while I watched my fair-haired savior run to catch up to her lanky girlfriend.

Marissa Lakeland. Why in the world did she have to be a witch? If she'd been a regular human, I could have started the process tonight. *Easily.* Just cleared her mind, made her expose her throat to me...

A groan escaped my lips, and her head jerked back as she looked in my direction. Her eyes, liquid pools of blue, gazed at the dark and the mist. I smiled. *She is as entranced by me as I am by her.*

My smile faded. The notion she wished to expose me for what I was instantly put a damper on our relationship. *Witch.*

The last time I had an unfortunate tangle with a teen witch, all I could do was croak out my exasperation. Even now, I could still sense the way my skin had felt—slimy, wet and cold, no longer smooth, but bumpy and a sickly brownish-green color. Really, I should have known to stay out of her path. My brother had warned me the witch had a strong aversion to humans, but being in one of my more cantankerous moods, I'd planned to show my brother how charming I could be and how the witch would delight in having a burger with me.

Right. For two hours I'd had to suffer the most horrible humiliation while my brother begged the witch to turn me back into my handsome self. The Hamburger Spot owner even demanded I be thrown out of his restaurant. But following that, I had to endure James berating me for a good part of the evening. I knew he'd never let me live it down. Thankfully, he never told Mom and Dad.

Only this time we couldn't hide my mistake from our parents. Under the dire circumstances, I felt they were holding up pretty well.

However, if I didn't solicit Marissa's help soon, I would be lost forever to the dark world of the undead. But would she help me? Her friend seemed surer of herself. Wouldn't she be a better choice?

No. Marissa was the one destined to be my savior. As soon as I saw the two girls at the burger joint, I knew. Her long, shiny blond hair caught my eye first. Her slim, trim figure, petite and cute as a pixie, next. But it was her eyes, alluring as the Caribbean waters, that captured my attention the most. Peering into them, I could see her every thought.

I chuckled. She thought I was handsome. Then I frowned. Expose me to the world as a vampire so she could get some warlock's attention? My canines itched to extend. Forever, she would be mine.

A witch. Why did she have to be a witch?

I kicked a leaf on the sidewalk. Why couldn't she have been a normal, everyday human girl? I glanced back at her form fading into the distance. Because for whatever reason, she was the one and only one who could save me—after all, it *was* written in the stars.

Dematerializing, I hurried after her. I had to learn everything I could about her. Where she lived, where she hung out, who her friends were.

Most of all, how best to make her mine.

Once I drew close to the girls again, the one Marissa called Kate turned to her and asked, "Why do you keep looking over your shoulder? Do you think he's following us?"

Marissa ran her hands over her silky shirtsleeves. "Don't you sense him too?"

She seemed slightly anxious, and my gut clenched to think I'd caused her to fear me. How could I convince her that she had to save me if she was afraid of me?

Kate surveyed the area, but she couldn't see me or feel my presence like Marissa could. That was another reason I knew Marissa was the right one. She and I had some kind of a connection—one that went beyond the physical. She sensed me, even if her eyes could not see me.

"There's no one there," Kate remarked, though her voice didn't sound sure at all. She picked up her pace again. "You're just jittery." She glanced at her watch. "And it's *way* past our bedtime." Heading down a walkway to a one-story, ranch-style home, she faced Marissa. "Are you going to be all right? I mean, you don't have far to reach your house, but your face is so...pale. Are you scared, Marissa?"

"No. I'm fine." Marissa vehemently shook her head and straightened her back. "See you in the morning for school."

"Yeah, don't dream anything I wouldn't tonight. Tall, dark, and handsome, sucking at your neck." Kate laughed at her own humor, though her tone of voice seemed somewhat tentative, then she hurried to her front door.

Marissa took a hesitant breath, then stalked off down the sidewalk. She took larger steps than I imagined she normally would take, her pace frenzied. Somehow, I had to put her at ease, but materializing in front of her wasn't the way. Still, I wanted to speak to her one more time before she disappeared into her home for the night. Actually, I wanted to kiss those turned down lips of hers and make her smile.

Then I wanted to bite her, and...

But rationally, I knew I needed to take it slowly with her. Not frighten her further. So what got into me to just pop in front of her like I did?

Patience definitely wasn't one of my virtues. I had to get her to agree to help me before it was too late. My time was running out. Besides, my impulsive nature hadn't been squashed when Lynetta turned me into a vampire.

A squeal issued from deep within Marissa's throat as soon as I appeared in front of her. I tried my most sensual smile, hoping it didn't appear too wickedly sinful. Feasting my eyes on her was pure delight, but my only intention was to calm her fears.

Her lips parted in surprise and her wide eyes showed her fright. I sensed her blood racing through her veins at lightning speed. Which definitely didn't help one bit when the rising bloodlust in my system compelled me to make her mine. Like the unfathomable addiction I had to chocolate, I couldn't help wanting her. Trying to curb my interest in her blood, I attempted to think of a way to soothe her frayed nerves, something I could say to calm her. How I wished she were human so I could use my vampiric charms on her and easily wipe the terror from her mind.

"What do you want with me?" she squeaked, her blue eyes barely blinking as if she were afraid I might suddenly vanish again.

However, her fairly calm response was a beginning. She didn't scream; she was talking to me.

"You draw me to you, Marissa. I can't help myself." I choked on the next words. "Can we be friends?"

We couldn't be just friends—not in the ordinary sense of the word. Lovers and mates forever, that's what we were destined to be. If only I could convince her to take the first step. If only she would give me her lifeblood…willingly, lovingly. If only—

She wrung her slender hands for a moment as if contemplating something, then having decided what she would do, she raised them. Wriggling her fingers at me, she silently spoke ancient words, her lips moving without speech.

Without my express permission, my lips turned up. Marissa really wasn't much like the other teen witch, I could see. Instead of using a dastardly spell on me, all she attempted was a defensive spell.

Her blond brows knit together. "What's so funny?" Her tone was angry, no longer fearful.

Good. I could deal with anger. Fear was harder to overcome, particularly when people learned what I was.

"Your spells…" I almost told her the truth. Her witch's spells wouldn't work on me, now that I was a vampire. At least I didn't think so, but if they made her feel more at ease, I would allow her to continue undisturbed.

Looking totally exasperated, she dropped her hands to her sides.

"Are you finished?" I didn't think she'd completed her spell.

Her actions indicated she hadn't finished her witch's training either. If she had, I wouldn't have so easily distracted her concentration with merely a smile. Grateful she had a heart and wasn't trying to cast a curse or hex on me, I took a ragged breath.

"If you're a—"

I folded my arms, trying to calm the outrage that slowly

burned inside of me, that the girl who would be my mate would wish to use me to catch a warlock. "You'll want to turn me into your witch's order. I'll be examined, poked and prodded, stripped naked, then put on display."

Her brows rose, and her full pink lips pursed. The notion I would be stripped of my clothes flitted across her mind, but I couldn't catch whether she felt this was a good thing, or bad. Then her lips turned up slightly. *Not good.*

I tried again to convince her of her folly. "Is that what you want? To prove to the others how you can take down a mighty Prince of Darkness?"

If nothing more, perhaps I could appeal to her sense of fairness.

She crossed her arms, her eyes still locked onto mine, but despite the revelation, she hid her feelings well. "So you *are* one."

I wasn't sure she truly believed I was, not unless I admitted it. "If you say so." I held out my hand to her, willing her to accept me for what I was, knowing my power to command her was futile. "Friends?"

Seemingly annoyed, she ignored my hand. "I don't want to turn you in to be poked, prodded, and put on display."

I didn't feel she was totally sincere, but it was a start. "But you want to prove I'm a Prince of Darkness. How else will you do it? Will anyone believe you without proof?"

She tilted her head to the side, her face still hiding any emotion. "Any suggestions?"

Inwardly, I smiled. Biting her would prove it. But if I suggested such a thing, would she run off screaming? The beat of her heart had slowed considerably but was still faster than normal. If I took a step toward her to close the gap between us, I was sure she would bolt.

Yet I could think of no other way to give her proof. If I'd been an ancient vampire, I might have had more ideas in mind. But that was the point. I wasn't and didn't want to suffer that fate. I wanted my life back, as much as it could return to normal. Marissa was the one to help me do it.

"Friends?" Again, I offered my hand, but she wouldn't draw near enough to take it. Risking everything, I said, "All right. If I bite you, would that be enough proof?"

She grinned. The prettiest, flashiest, brilliantly white toothy grin I've ever seen. Perfect teeth in size, shape and color. She could be a model for a toothpaste commercial, or orthodontistry work or something. The best thing was she hadn't run away or taken a step back, and her face wasn't filled with anxiety or horror.

Standing taller, she asked in an amused voice, "Bite me?"

Though the upturned lilt in her tone at the end of her words indicated she'd asked a question, I took full advantage of stating otherwise. "Are you asking me to?" I knew she wasn't, but I still had to hope, fool that I was. If only she would allow me to, it would end all of my miserable fleeting moments of worrying whether I would get out of the horrible predicament I was in.

Not that it wasn't my fault. I should never have kissed the girl that I did, siren that she was—ancient vampire that she was. I groaned at my folly.

Teach me to pick up any old girl before I knew more of who she was and where she'd been.

Marissa's eyes sparkled with amusement, and her dimples grew even bigger. "No, I didn't offer for you to bite me. I..." She smiled a little. "I was repeating what I thought you'd said. That's your only suggestion of my proving you're a—"

"Prince of Darkness," I interrupted, stopping her from saying the hated vampire word. Though that one wasn't nearly as awful as the bloodsucker term.

When the breeze flipped her sun-streaked curls into her

eyes, she swept them out of her face. "Prince of Darkness. Can't you think of any other way to prove you exist?"

"Afraid not. I've only just been turned, and..." I was dying to tell her the truth, but why would someone who didn't even know me choose to risk her life to aid me? Somehow, I had to use my charms to convince her to allow me to bite her, but how could I, with her being a witch? I sighed heavily. In a week's time, I would lose all chance at a reversal.

She waited patiently for me to finish what I had to say.

Hoping to show my anguish and the awful predicament I was in, I pinched my brows together, attempting my most woeful look.

Her smile faded, but a glimmer of it stayed on her lips. Either she thought I was the worst actor she had ever witnessed, or she thought I was a great comedian.

"If you help me, I can become human again. But I only have until Friday. At midnight, I will remain what I am forever, a shadow of the night."

Her facial expression didn't change, yet I felt she was still amused by what I had to say. "What would I need to do?" she asked, businesslike.

Hope flickered while I rubbed my neck to reduce the tension in my taut muscles. "You have to share your blood with me." At least that was part of the deal. I didn't dare tell her the rest this early on. One baby step at a time.

She shook her head, definitely opposed. Not good. "Then you could turn me into what you are."

"Not while I'm still only partly turned. It's the only way." Though I hadn't meant to grovel, my tone of voice definitely pleaded with her. Would she take pity?

I couldn't spring the second part of the equation on her. Not yet. First, the blood swap. If she wouldn't agree to it, nothing else mattered. Then, well, killing the one who was turning me would have to be accomplished next. That would end the spell. But Marissa had to do the killing. As my true mate, she was the only one who could save me.

She inhaled deeply. "I'll sleep on it." She headed down the sidewalk toward her house.

I couldn't stop the way my heart took a dive. I didn't want to try again the next day—each hour that passed brought me closer to a permanent hell I wanted to avoid at all costs. I had to convince her to agree, at least to the first step. "Nobody but you can save me, Marissa. You're the only one."

She visibly swallowed hard. At least I knew she was considering it. Even if she wasn't totally agreeable, she hadn't turned me down outright.

I followed her as she drew closer to the wraparound porch of her two-story colonial home. I sensed no one was home, which was a good thing for me, but not for her. Why would her parents leave her home alone? Maybe she was more responsible than I ever was. Of course, things had changed considerably since I'd been turned. "Is there nothing else I can say or do to convince you?"

She stopped and turned to face me, an impish smile tugging at her lips. "Take me to the school dance."

I hesitated, absolutely thrown off balance by her demand. I couldn't dance, not even at the best of times. On the other hand, did it mean she was willing to let me have a taste of her blood?

"A witches' and warlocks' affair?" I asked, trying to keep my tone neutral, but the nervousness still sounded in my voice. I had two left feet, and both had stepped on my date's sandaled feet the only time I'd ever gotten brave enough to take a girl to a dance. Word soon spread, and no girl, no matter how charmingly I asked, would go with me to a dance following that disaster.

"Yes. Take me to it. I haven't been asked yet." Marissa walked backwards up the brick path to her house, her mind made up, her eyes sparkling with interest.

Immediately, a sense of relief washed over me. I was off the hook. "I can't, can I? Not unless I'm a warlock."

She narrowed her eyes.

I couldn't imagine as pretty as Marissa was that she wouldn't already have a date, but I also knew if I could have, I should have jumped at the chance to take her if it meant she would share her blood with me. My reluctance? The niggling worry that I would dance on her feet when she was to be my permanent mate was the problem. But because I wasn't a warlock the issue was moot anyway. Though now I was once again faced with trying to persuade her to go along with my plan. "I would think you would have to turn a lot of guys down."

She grinned at me, showing off those perfect teeth once again. "I guess I was saving my dances for you. But...you're right. You can't get in unless you're a warlock. I guess I was just so hopeful...I forgot."

She looked awfully disappointed, and I felt like a real heel for being grateful I couldn't attend. Yet I couldn't change what I was, nor could I modify the rules of the witches' and warlocks' dance.

I had hooked her—if only I could take her to the dance. "What about a movie or breakfast?" Dinner out could be a little too dangerous.

"I would rather you could take me to the dance," she said, folding her arms.

Not good. Then another thought hit me. Why was she so stuck on me taking her to the dance? Was it a trick to get me in front of the witch's tribunal? My enthusiasm that she wished to help me suddenly deflated like a needle-pricked bubble.

A stirring in the air behind me warned me of impending doom and filled me with anguish. The devil vamp had returned for more of my blood and if I didn't save Marissa, the vamp would make short work of her.

"Lynetta," I cried out, panic in my voice, trying to distract the vampiress. Marissa stood only a few steps away from her front door. She could make it if she bolted for it now. "Run into your house, Marissa!"

I couldn't let Lynetta catch her. No telling what the vengeful vampire might do to her. No matter what, I needed Marissa to help me win against the devil. The notion a girl could help me still didn't quite sit well with me, but I was coming to grips with the idea I needed her more than life itself.

Lynetta swooped toward Marissa with the speed of a hawk. I dove in between the two, attempting to delay Lynetta's stab at tackling Marissa.

I sensed Marissa hesitate behind me when Lynetta grabbed my throat with one of her hands. She clasped her long, wicked fingers around my wrists with her other hand, binding me at once to her will.

"Run, Marissa!" I croaked, Lynetta's strong fingers sealing off the air to my windpipe to make me behave. With all my heart, my only hope was that Marissa would get away and never see what Lynetta had in mind to do with me next.

3

Marissa

"Watch well, witch," the woman called back to me as she squeezed Dominic's throat. Dressed in a black spandex shirt, matching jeans and a pair of high-heeled, thigh-high boots, she looked like a regular teen.

My heart lodged in my throat while my blood turned to ice, but I wouldn't run and hide.

"See what I will do to you next!" She turned her attention to Dominic. "Do you think a scrawny thing like her can kill me? Do you? She's trembling in her sneakers as we speak. Well, as *I* speak."

I froze to the concrete sidewalk, unsure what to do next to save Dominic from the vampire. I wanted to pound her into the ground, but the way she held Dominic tightly in her grasp, I knew I couldn't physically best her. I suspected none of my spells would work against an ancient vampire, and though the woman looked only to be my age, seventeen, she seemed older than time in her actions and speech.

She leaned over and licked Dominic's cheek, and his expression turned from concern for me to hatred for her.

None of Dominic's own words had emotionally stirred me to save him like the unbridled actions of the vampire at his throat. Lynetta bared her wickedly sharp pointed canines and hissed. Her long black hair hung wildly to her hips, tangled and teased by the breeze. She was petite like me, but as strong as a male bodybuilder, her grip on Dominic remaining iron tight. Her soulless black eyes, vacant and without a care, really ate away at my heart.

I surveyed the yard for any kind of weapon I could use against the vampire. My heart surged when I spied a colorful whirligig attached to a wooden stake embedded in my mother's pampered pansy garden nearby. Without a second's hesitation, I dashed for it and yanked it out.

Running at the vampire, I screamed at the top of my lungs, "Death to the bloodsucking vampire!" Which gave me some courage. It wasn't every day I had to beat one vampire off another, when they didn't even really exist. Who would ever thought I would have to tell Kate she was so right?

All I could think of was aiming the stake at the vampire's heart—at least that's what the books said would work on them —except Lynetta used Dominic to shield her. I ground my teeth, dancing around them, taking aim at the vamp anywhere that I could strike, praying I wouldn't hit Dominic by accident.

With great relief, I thwarted her enough that she was unable to bite him, and I imagined she thought of me as a pesky, insignificant gnat, just as hard to strike down while she was trying to maintain her grip on Dominic. She snarled in anger, baring her fangs at me. My heart raced, sending the blood coursing through my system while I concentrated on striking the vampire again and again.

But the distressing notion kept running through my mind, *I am a failure*. I had messed up tons of potions and spells at school, caused an explosion in the lab, and turned a teacher into a baboon. How could someone as inept as me save Dominic from this fiend? Why didn't he find another witch who had top honors, like Kate, to help him? By choosing me, he'd sealed his fate.

Yet, for now, he had no one else to aid him and I had to squash the sense of hopelessness that ate away at my confidence. I would save him...somehow.

Dominic struggled to get free, and I assumed Lynetta's grip on him had loosened while I distracted her. Gritting my teeth, I struck the stake at her shoulder as hard as I could, all the while chanting ancient words, "*Malachon, revelist, baraths, chalmeon!*"

She screamed out in pain, but the stake wasn't sharp enough to cut her. Now on me, I would have bruises the size of Texas, but I wondered if a vampire would bruise that easily.

"Witch's spells won't work on me, you little...little witch!" she yelled at me.

I couldn't help smiling at the way she called me a witch in such a derogatory way, which meant she was losing her cool and I was winning some of the game. In our dancing back and forth, my attempts to strike the vampire and Dominic's struggles to get free, I moved us closer to the edge of my front porch. If we could reach my house, I would invite him in. The vampire couldn't get to him then, at least for the time being, I didn't think.

Suddenly, Dominic broke loose, grabbed my arm, and shoved me to the door. "Do it!" he shouted, as if he thought I knew all the rules about being a vampire. Maybe the books were right.

I screamed back, "Come in, Dominic!"

I fumbled with the key in the lock, then jerked the door open. Dominic wrenched himself free and dove in, carrying me with him.

Both of us fell on the tiled entryway, but Dominic managed to break my fall with heroic effort. Lynetta hissed at the doorway, baring her fangs. The look she gave us was like she was the Medusa herself—minus the writhing snakes shooting out of her head, but able to turn a body to stone anyway.

Dominic jumped to his feet and slammed the door in her face. "Your parents?" he whispered and helped me to my feet.

His touch was warm and caring and instantly heated my cold, clammy hands. "Away on a trip to Mexico, celebrating their eighteenth wedding anniversary. A witch at seventeen is considered responsible enough to leave alone. Besides, my Aunt Betsy lives two houses down if I have any trouble."

His dark brows furrowed. "Trouble like me."

Taking a deep settling breath, I touched the bruises already discoloring his throat in shades of black and blue. "I'm sure no one in my family would have expected me to have *this* kind of trouble, but for your own safety, you can stay here until Friday. How is your throat? Can I—"

"One of the advantages of being..." His words trailed off for a second, then he cleared his gravelly throat. "We heal at accelerated rates."

"Oh." I tried to keep my reaction neutral when it came to discussing his—differences, but I'm sure my eyes widened a little.

He kept his distance, though we only stood an arm's length away, yet he seemed to want to draw closer. Finally, he said, "I want to thank you for your help, Marissa. Only my lifemate would have been able to rescue me."

Although gladdened he felt I was so useful, I really didn't

feel that way about my capabilities. I'd been lucky, that's all. "I couldn't let her hurt you, Dominic."

"Because we're connect—"

Silencing him with a shake of my head, I did not want to hear anything more about our fate being written in the stars. I didn't believe it for one instant. Witches married warlocks and that was that. Any that made the mistake of marrying a human diluted the magical abilities in their gene pool, and their mixed children suffered. Though, my magic wasn't all that great, and both my parents were magic users—guess it went to show there was a dud in every bunch. Still, the idea of marrying a vampiric human was scandalous. What kind of children would that spawn? Or would it even be possible? And why was I even thinking about such a thing?

He gently rubbed his wrists where Lynetta had savagely gripped him. "Where can I sleep?"

"Do you have to sleep with your dirt? Or a coffin?"

At the notion, he grimaced. "A room without rays of sunlight filtering in will do. And no, I don't sleep with a pile of dirt." He shook his head. "Old wives' tales."

"You can sleep in the guestroom next to mine. It's all frilly and purple, but the only other bedroom is my parents' and—"

The phone rang, jangling my already frayed nerves. I grabbed the phone and read the Caller ID. "My Aunt Betsy," I whispered as if she could hear me. I punched the on button. "Hello?"

"Marissa. I've been worried sick about you."

"Oh, I'm so sorry, Aunt Betsy. You know Kate. She led me on a wild goose chase searching for vampires." I winked at Dominic, and he smiled back at me. He had the most gorgeous smile, but not a tooth too big or wicked at all, making me wonder where he kept his fangs tucked away.

Silence met my ear, and I knew at once something was

wrong. My aunt had never been a worrywart, in fact I was lucky that none of my family had that dysfunction. "Aunt Betsy?"

"Something killed five humans and drained the blood from them. The police are trying to keep everyone from panicking. They're saying it's some sicko pretending to be a vampire."

My blood chilled and I stared at Dominic. Could he have been in on the killings?

He folded his arms and shook his head.

I gulped, my thoughts a jumble while I considered what I'd been thinking earlier when I'd first spied him. Had he read my mind?

He nodded, a small smile curving his lips and a glitter of amusement sparkling in his dark brown eyes.

My heart dropped ten stories. Jeez, what in the world had I said—*no*, not said, but thought—about him?

"Marissa? Are you still there, dear?" Aunt Betsy's concerned voice brought me crashing back to earth.

I swallowed hard, but my throat had dried up like Texas did in the middle of a drought-ridden summer. "Uhm, yes, okay, well, uhm, we'll be extra careful, and it's getting really late so I need to—"

"You and Kate aren't to go out at night without a proper chaperone until the criminal is caught," Aunt Betsy warned.

I looked at Dominic, wondering if he knew who the killer was. How many vampiric creatures hidden under the cover of night stalked new victims? Never in a millennium did I realize chasing after a cute guy late at night would turn into a sinister game of chance. "All right, well, I've got school tomorrow, so—"

"Did you need me to come over and tuck you in?"

"No!" My heart thudded. "I mean, nobody's done that to me since I was little. I *am* seventeen."

"It was a figure of speech, dear. I didn't want you to be afraid to be by yourself."

I was losing it. Slowly, I let out my breath. "No, I'll be fine."

"Okay, then, Marissa. Call me when you get home from school tomorrow. Goodnight, dear."

"Night, Aunt Betsy." I hung up the phone, worried I'd made a grave mistake by inviting Dominic into my parents' home. What was worse, I now knew he could read my thoughts!

"Most of the time, Marissa." Dominic rubbed his smooth chin, his face an emotionless mask. "Sometimes, when you're stressed, your thoughts get a little jumbled and it's hard to read them."

I groaned, my mind shifting through a million different notions. What in the world had I been thinking of him? My cheeks heated when I considered him being stripped naked. Never had I seen a boy naked before, well, except for Cousin Jimmy, but he was only an infant and Aunt Betsy was changing his diaper and...

Dominic grinned.

My body temperature grew to sauna levels, and I folded my arms in exasperation. "Quit reading my thoughts!"

"Sorry. I can't help myself." He cocked a brow, devilishly sensual and totally unnerving.

"Can you read Kate's?"

He shook his head. "No. I can read only yours. That's why I know you're the one for me."

Great. Most of the time I could control my tongue, but my thoughts, too? It would be like walking along the edge of a crumbling cliff. Unless I was stressed out an awful lot, I would have to start curbing my thoughts around him. Then I considered what my aunt had said. "Did you hear how there have been several killings in the area?"

"Yes. When you thought about your aunt's comments, I read your mind. You wondered if I had anything to do with them. I did not. The only one I've fed off is Lynetta. Until she's turned me completely, I'm not supposed to feed off anything or anyone else."

"*Anything* else?"

"Mammals. Anything with warm, red blood."

My stomach churning, I made a face. "And me?"

"I'll bond to you instead. Since you are truly my intended, she won't be able to break us apart once we've bonded."

I walked into the living room and collapsed on the soft blue velvet sofa. The ceiling fan spun around overhead, the way my mind was spinning. Motioning to the couch, I offered Dominic to take a seat. "Is that all there is to it?"

To my guarded relief, he kept a pillow's distance between us when he sat down next to me. I still wasn't sure I trusted him.

For a moment, he stared at the fireplace mantle covered with family pictures, then he turned to me. "You have to kill her. It's the only way to release me from her grasp permanently."

My mouth dropped open. Sure, the sick creature appeared evil to the core, and sure, I thought we would all be better off if she disappeared from the earth forever, but *I* had to kill her? With mediocre witch's skills, not even a sliver of the vamp's physical strength, and not half as fearless as the wicked creature —*I* had to kill her? Dominic couldn't have surprised me anymore if he'd told me that he wasn't my supposed lifemate but my long-lost brother instead.

He smiled.

I frowned, wishing he would quit reading my mind, at the same time chiding myself for not remembering to watch my thoughts better. "You didn't tell me that part." I wondered how in the world I'd gotten myself into this mess. No, Kate. After all, *she* was the one who made me chase after Dominic in the first place. As for me, I had been content to sip a chocolate milkshake at the burger place. I studied Dominic's intense gaze and sensed him pleading with me to agree. "And if I don't kill her?"

"She'll turn me all the way." He ran his hand over the soft sofa. "I'm afraid once I'm turned, I'll still want you for my own. We're meant to be together. Only I won't be able to control myself once I've been fully turned."

I felt as if I'd slipped into a very deep well, and there was no way to fight my way out of the blackness. "Great."

Why couldn't he have wanted Debbie Damint, the hottest blonde bombshell at school? She had perfect school scores, perfect nails—I glanced quickly down at my fingernails, broken and chipped as usual—beautiful figure, great in sports, had tons of girlfriends and boyfriends. She was the girl I loved to hate most.

"Nope, not Debbie Damint." His lips curved up while his eyes sparkled with amusement.

"You haven't even seen her. All the guys make fools of themselves over her."

"There's only one whom I desire to make a fool of myself over."

Were all vampires as charming as Dominic? Did they get a special class in it?

"You bring it out in me, Marissa."

"Quit reading my thoughts!" Jeez, I really had to concentrate on keeping him out of my mind.

The grin still tugged at his lips.

"Okay," I said, hoping to change the subject again. "So if I don't help you, she turns you into a full-fledged vampire, and you'll be able to get into my house anytime you want? Great, now what have I done? The first time my parents ever let me stay home alone, and I have screwed up big time."

"If you kill her, all will be well," he said, as if he were telling me I could bake a batch of chocolate chip cookies, which, for all of my other failings, I was very good at if I say so myself.

But this was not about cooking. Unless I cooked the vamp,

somehow. "Jeez, Dominic. How in the world am I going to be able to kill her? I'm not very good at witch's spells."

His fingers drew closer to me, as if he were reaching out, trying to console me for feeling so inadequate. "You not only distracted Lynetta, the spell you chanted bothered her enough that she began to loosen her grip on my wrists." His words were said with pride, and he even puffed out his chest a little.

The spell had worked after all? Wow. I'd had Kate confine my wrists so I could practice the incantation, but I didn't think I'd really mastered it. The spell was great for self-defense, if I could get the hang of it in a pinch—which considering how it helped Dominic, I guess I had learned it all right.

"You used a release spell, didn't you?" His eyes still showed great admiration.

"Yes, I did." So, he wasn't disappointed that I was a witch after all? Most humans didn't really want to get involved with them.

"You saved me," Dominic simply said.

Partially satisfied, I nodded. Though I couldn't understand why the vamp hadn't fully released him then.

"She's an ancient and awfully powerful. Plus, you're not a fully trained witch, are you?"

That bothered me. Again, I wondered why he didn't seek out a witch with greater abilities. It wouldn't be hard to find one. "No, I'm not fully trained. We all advance at different rates. Uhm…" I clutched my fingers together and couldn't look at him, but I thought he should know the truth. "Some say I'm a, well, a…" I hated to say what others teased me mercilessly about, "…a slow learner."

He shrugged as if to indicate it didn't mean anything to him but seemed anxious about what to say to console me. Finally, he reached out and touched my hand. "Yeah, but they don't have lifemates whose destinies are written in the stars."

I wanted to groan out loud. I was a slow learner and was to be mated with a vampiric human whose old flame wanted me dead. How was this a good thing? "So then, how do you propose I kill her?"

"When we begin to bond, you will gain some of my strength...some of my abilities."

"Great. I can grow hair on my chest."

He laughed out loud.

The sound of his hearty, well-meaning laughter cheered me. He laughed with me, not at me like some of the other boys did.

He squeezed my hand. "They're idiots, Marissa. Will you help me? Save me from a fate worse than death? Will you?"

If I helped him, would it be the dumbest thing I ever did? Or the bravest? Or maybe a little of both? Still, could I do it?

I considered Dominic's mournful look. Killing an ancient vampire would prove impossible, wouldn't it? And the idea of Dominic's sucking my blood and my sucking his...I shuddered.

I cleared my throat. "If I agree to allow you to bite me..."

A flicker of interest showed in Dominic's dark eyes.

"*If*..." I repeated, "what new powers might I possess?"

4

D OMINIC

MARISSA SAT BESIDE ME, the most stunning girl I had ever known. Her shiny hair begged for my caress. Her full pink lips waited for my kiss. Even her silky blue shirt touched her beautiful breasts the way I wanted to. And her eyes...clear blue and full of intrigue. Not filled with fright or condemnation but with genuine interest.

Was it because she was my soul mate that she caused my molecules to shift so suddenly every time she drew near? Or the human part of my maleness that desired her with fervent longing? Or the vampiric bloodlust that urged me to take her blood and make her mine forever?

I attempted to focus on convincing her how right we were for each other.

"As a Prince of Darkness, I can do many things. Appear in places I've been before, materializing in a form of mist, or full-bodied. Just like when I popped in front of you, Marissa, or like when I appeared in a shadowy form near the trees."

Her gaze never wavering from mine, she listened intently.

What I feared most was if I shared my blood with her, my own abilities would diminish. If I wasn't strong enough, could I fight Lynetta at all then? Or would Marissa gain some of my abilities, without draining me of them? I wasn't sure of anything.

Gritting my teeth, I tried to calm my concern. "As a mist, I can whisper words and see and hear what goes on around me. And in a tight fix, unless Lynetta has hold of me, I can vanish, then reappear elsewhere."

Of course, the drawback was I needed blood from time to time to replenish my own. Since I hadn't fed on Lynetta this evening, I was sure to be weaker by morning. If that happened, I wouldn't stand a chance against her as soon as dusk fell.

"Anything else, Dominic?" Marissa leaned forward on the couch, intently listening to my every word.

Was she always this enthusiastic a listener, or did my tale intrigue her more than most?

"I can see everything in the dark as if the sun had never set. I can hear sounds humans can't hear. And I can fly to the top of a tree or roof or climb the flat side of a building with ease."

Marissa smiled. The tension I was feeling in every sinew eased a bit.

"Neat." Then she wrung her hands and her brow wrinkled. "What's the downside?"

"Sensitivity to sunlight. I can still manage in the daylight, particularly if it's overcast. But on a bright sunny day, I'm better off staying inside. My skin easily burns as if I'd been in the midday sun for hours trying to get a tan."

"What about food?"

"I still eat human food. I was enjoying a cheeseburger when I spied you at the Hamburger Spot."

"But you need blood?"

I couldn't lie to her. If she were to help me through this ordeal, we had to be partners. "I have to tell you by not feeding on Lynetta tonight, I'll be weaker by morning. I imagine I won't have the strength to free myself from her by tomorrow night when she comes for me again if she catches me outside your home."

"So..." Marissa swallowed hard, and I could sense she was coming to a decision, probably one of the most difficult she would ever have to make. "If I let you bite me"—she shuddered —"you wouldn't be weak, or as weak, but I still wouldn't have to drink your blood? I mean, it would be like I would give a donation at the blood bank, right?"

"Yes. As long as you don't drink my blood, you won't experience any change. Well, you might be a little light-headed, but you won't be any worse off than that." She was going to do it, my brave mate. My heart lifted.

"It's just the idea that you would sink those pointed fangs into me like Lynetta threatened you with..."

I wished she hadn't seen that, but then again, if she hadn't, we might not be sitting on her couch right now, working up to the first step in my salvation. "We'll work up slowly to it...by kissing first," I tried reassuring her.

Marissa's lips turned up considerably. "Now Kate would say that was a guy line if she ever heard one."

I couldn't help but smile. From the thoughts I gathered from her, she'd never been kissed before. At least she couldn't compare me with anyone else. But the real question was would she go along with it?

My only other worry was whether I could stop once I fed on her blood. Lynetta always halted me when I'd had enough. Could I tell when I'd had my fill of Marissa and not harm her? No way did I want to hurt my soul mate.

Marissa ran her hand over the couch. "What do I have to do? I'm not saying I'm going through with this, but if I did, what would be the steps?"

"I would have to move closer to you, like this." I scooted closer, our knees touching. I feared that I would scare her away, but already the bloodlust was rising in my system. Mainly because I hadn't fed in twenty-four hours, and partly because her special warm blood called to me...my mate's blood.

Already I could hear her blood coursing faster in her veins, which urged me to feed even more, but at the same time I knew I had to try to keep her from panicking. "At any time if you feel uncomfortable, stop me, Marissa. I don't want to upset you."

"Proceed," she said, her word spoken quickly as if she was afraid she would change her mind if she didn't take the plunge right away.

Her back was so stiff, I knew if I were to ever drink her blood, I would have to get her to relax or hurt her in the process.

"If you were a regular human, I could calm your fears and get you to relax. But since I can't, I'll have to try to relax you with my voice and words. I'm not sure I can." Despite trying to project a confident image, I sounded like I thought I might lose the battle.

"Go ahead and try. I'll attempt to loosen up." Her muscles tightened when I took her hand in mine.

"Do you know any self-hypnosis?"

"I guess I'm tensing too much." She took several deep calming breaths, then tensed her muscles and relaxed them, repeating the steps several times.

The pulse in her wrist slowed to normal. I nodded, grateful that Marissa was such a treasure despite my initial concern she might be more like the teen witch who had turned me into a frog. "Much better."

I leaned over to kiss her lips, but she thrust her hand into my chest, and I bit back a laugh. "You can stop, can't you? You won't go too far, will you?"

Taking her hand, I kissed it. "Do what you did just then—shove me away, or tell me to stop, and I'll cease and desist." At least I hoped I could.

She relaxed against the sofa cushions. "Okay."

I leaned over her again, my gaze focused on her full pink lips, lightly moistened by the flick of her tongue.

"Boy, if my parents knew what I was up to."

Trying to ignore her nervous chatter, I kissed her mouth with the faintest touch. Her blue eyes grew wide with worry. "Relax, Marissa. It's only the briefest of kisses." This was going to be a lot harder than I ever imagined possible. We would never get anywhere if she wouldn't relax, and again I wished—somewhat guiltily this time—that she was only human.

"You mean, they get worse, I mean harder, I mean—"

"Better." I held her hands, caressing them gently, but not in a confining manner. I tilted my face up to her eyes and kissed one eyelid then the other, forcing her to close her eyes, bringing a smile to her lips. Running my finger over them, I whispered, "You have the prettiest smile I have ever seen."

Her smile spread. She kept her eyes closed, but her breathing grew more rapid. Again, her anxiety mounted.

"Just a kiss," I whispered against her mouth. I touched her throat with my fingers. The throb of her pulse, her warm blood flowing sweetly through her veins, urged me on. Giddy with desire, I kissed her lips more firmly, trying to keep my fangs from extending too soon, trying to show how kind, caring, giving I could be, before I took from her what I craved.

"Marissa," I whispered next to her cheek.

She stroked my arm, encouraging me to lull her into a state of bliss. I licked her neck, and she tilted her head to the side, exposing her throat to me, offering her lifeblood. In return for what? To save my life? Someone she hadn't even known before tonight?

Beyond a doubt, she was my savior.

My control over them lost, my teeth extended. If she pushed me away now, changed her mind, could I stop?

Propelling me onward, like a man lost in the desert searching for his salvation, the bloodlust raged out of control. The madness threatened to shove me into the darkest abyss, a bottomless pit of despair. If she stopped me, I feared I would die of hunger, of rejection, of the knowledge I would be a Prince of Darkness forever.

She pulled me closer. She wanted me to feast on her as much as I longed to, and yet I worried I would hurt or repulse her. I grazed my teeth along the soft skin of her neck. She shivered and swallowed hard. Her hands tightened on my shoulders, keeping me close, not pushing me away. My teeth punctured the skin. She gasped. I couldn't delay. If she didn't stop me now...

Too late.

I sucked her warm blood tasting like sweet copper and quickly nourished my depleted body.

She leaned back against the sofa, her body finally relaxing, but her fingers still held me close. If I wasn't careful, I could take too much of her blood. My hunger held me to her throat like a vine clung to a wall for support. Strengthened and warmed by her blood, I finally had to force myself to withdraw my teeth, then licked the tiny puncture wounds to seal them.

Then my cell phone vibrated in my pants pocket. To my utter annoyance, I bit my tongue and cursed inwardly. Shoving my hand into my pocket, I found the phone and turned it off.

Marissa stared back at me, her eyes darkened, her lips slightly parted. I kissed them again, only this time I touched my tongue to hers, only wanting to kiss her deeply, not for any other purpose than to show my profound gratitude, my love for her. I hadn't any dark purpose in mind, nor had I planned to trick her into accepting me.

But the deed was done.

I hadn't realized at first a trickle of the blood on my tongue was not hers, but mine. When her tongue tangled with mine, she unwittingly received some of my blood.

Would she hate me for not having given her the choice? Worst of all, now what would happen? If I turned her, though I still felt it wouldn't be possible since I hadn't been fully turned myself, how could she help me? And how could I help her likewise?

I tried to break free from the kiss, but she held me firm. Like a siren of the sea, she had caught her drowning sailor and carried me to the heavens above. Inwardly, I smiled. For being a neophyte kisser, she certainly had learned how to completely cast a spell over me.

Not wanting to break the kiss, I still felt obligated to tell her the truth, hoping beyond hope she wouldn't hate me now. I finally managed to pull away but pressed my lips against her cheek as a parting goodnight kiss.

"The bite marks will disappear by tomorrow, most likely." I was nearly sure of this because my healing capabilities were much advanced as a Prince of Darkness. Now that she had some of my blood...

I silently groaned, exasperated with myself. How could I have let it happen?

She reached up and touched the bite marks.

Trying to avoid thinking of what I might have done to her, I gave her a small smile. "They look like some guy gave you a couple of good hickeys."

Not amused, she frowned. "Kate will be sure to ask me where I got them from."

"What will you say?"

"I'm not sure. I'll have to think on it." Taking my hand, she kissed it. "When can I give blood to you again?"

I groaned outwardly this time. I'd created a monster. Touching her cheek, I gazed into her beautiful blue eyes. "I take it I didn't hurt you."

"It was the most exhilarating experience I've ever had...like a heated shower just poured over me, touching every molecule in my body, warming me from the inside out."

Delighted she'd enjoyed our blood bonding as much as she had, as much as I had, I squeezed her hand to reassure her that I'd felt just as alive with her touch. I sighed deeply, wanting to tell her what I'd done. "Marissa, I have to tell you—"

"Hmmm, was it as good for you as it was for me?" She stroked my arm again, and I wanted to devour every bit of her right then and there.

"You are truly fine."

Her face suddenly clouded. "Better than Lynetta?"

A scourge of bitterness attacked my gut just thinking about that vamp. "There's no comparison. Where you are the sugar in a sweet and sour mix, she is the tart. Where you are the warmth of the sunshine on a Florida summer day, she is the icy darkness in frigid Antarctica. You, and only you, are meant to be the one for me."

And now that we'd swapped blood, she had no choice. It would be forever.

5

MARISSA

KISSING DOMINIC HAD BEEN the most profound experience I'd ever had. Every fiber of my being had been on high alert, anxious about his taking my blood. But when he bit me, it was nothing more than a pricking sensation, and then oh so sweet. For once in my life, I, Marissa, ordinary witch who'd never caught a guy's eye, was loved. Yeah, by a vampire.

But what a vampire...Prince of Darkness, rather. Hmmm, what if I told Kate I had found my very own prince?

Dominic smiled.

I forgot he could read my thoughts, and immediately my face heated with embarrassment. "I guess if you've fed enough, it's really time for me to get to bed. I've got to go to school early."

"Show me the way, princess of my dreams."

Feeling extremely tired, I led him up the stairs that seemed to grow longer with every step. A charmer, that's what he was. I loved how he seemed to cherish me. But had he been like that before the vampire got hold of him?

"I've always liked girls, if that's what you mean. You know, the kind of guy who preferred talking to girls over fighting a guy at recess like so many of the clowns did."

"Ahhhh. Been a lot of girls, have there?"

He chuckled behind me.

After leading him down the hallway, I opened the door to the guest bedroom.

"One too many girls," he finally said. "The last nearly did me in. Guess I should have stuck to proving how macho I could be fighting the guys."

He joked as if it didn't bother him, but I could tell from the wrinkle of his brow and soulful eyes, he hung on to a thread of a life he so longed to have back.

"You will return to the way you were, right after we're through with her, right?"

"One of the other vamps hinted I would be much better off. I assumed I would get my regular life back."

Pain squeezed my heart like a symbiotic reaction. I leaned over and kissed his cheek, wondering how he had won me over in an instant. *Lynetta.* I could still envision her soulless eyes narrowed at me and her teeth bared. Even now, chill bumps trailed down my arms, and I shuddered. I knew I had to save him.

Touching my shoulders, he leaned over, then kissed my lips. "Goodnight, sweet angel of mercy."

The heartrending tenderness of his gaze nearly undid me. Not wanting him to have any illusions that I was some perfect angel, I warned, "I can be really cranky if I don't get enough sleep."

Amusement flickered across his face. "Until we wake, then."

Stepping into the dark room, he didn't turn on the light. He didn't need to, I belatedly realized, and I wondered if the changes had come easily to him, or if he'd had to adjust to them. I shut the door, my mind groggy but full of questions.

Morning would come way too soon.

I headed down the hall to my room and stepped inside. It took me some time to realize in the middle of my changing into an oversized T-shirt, that Dominic was speaking in the room next to me.

My heart plummeted while the blood in my veins burst into overdrive. Had he let Lynetta in after all? Had she willed him to do so?

I ran for the guest bedroom and jerked the door open. Dominic sat on the edge of the bed, wearing only a pair of black satin boxers decorated in bright red lips while he spoke into a cell phone.

I gulped to see him nearly naked, and me wearing only a T-shirt. "Sorry," I whispered, wondering what in the world I thought I would have done had I found Lynetta in the room with him. Slapped her silly?

He winked at me, then took in my appearance and grinned. "Yes, Mom, I'll be at a friend's. I'll be safe for tonight. Call you tomorrow." He snapped the phone shut. "Did you need another goodnight kiss?" Looking sinfully wicked, he smiled again.

I pointed back to my room. "I worried when I heard voices in here." I poked a loose curl dangling at my cheek behind my ear, feeling guilty for thinking badly of him. "You...you have a mother?"

His mouth quirked with humor. "Yep. And a father, too. Every kid normally has one of each to begin with."

He was teasing me in an affectionate way, and I realized how ridiculous I must sound. "I...I never thought that you might have a family nearby. You didn't tell them about me? About...us?"

"I don't want to get their hopes up. They're still pretty shaken up about this. Afraid the human population would want my head on a stake, or under the knife to figure out how I became this way, my parents intend to keep my secret. They told my high school that I was injured in a bad accident, and I would be homeschooled the rest of the year. I can't see any of my friends now. Everything has to be kept a big secret."

Not knowing what else to say, I nodded. I could just imagine my parents' upset if I had been turned. But I couldn't imagine how hard it must be for him to have to give up his friends and live a life of secrecy like this. "Can Lynetta get into your house?"

"No. I met her at the Hamburger Spot."

"And you still go there?"

"Best grilled burgers in town." He winked, his eyes full of mirth.

I wondered how he could take his situation with such good humor. I didn't think I would be able to fare as well. Stepping back in the direction of the doorway, I wished I could help him regain his former state of being, instantly. But for now, I had to get out of the guest bedroom where a nearly naked male vampire sat on the purple ruffled bed. "I'll see you tomorrow."

"Sweet dreams."

"Uhm, yes. Well, you too."

I hurried out of the guestroom, wondering if he had seen the blush rise to my cheeks as hot as they'd become when I saw him so undressed. But when I reached my bedroom, a horrible thought filled my brain. If he could see me in the dark, that was normal for him, being that he was a vampire and all. But I hadn't turned on the light to see him. In fact, when I changed into my nightshirt in my own bedroom, and even now when I walked through the hallway, I hadn't turned on any of the lights.

Walking into my bedroom, I reached up and flipped up the

light switch. The lights glowed but didn't further illuminate the bedroom.

"Dominic!" I screamed, anger filling every cell of my body.

Instantly, he appeared at my doorway. A look of puzzlement stretched across his face. He seemed totally unaware of what had happened to me.

"What's wrong, Marissa? I feared the worst—that Lynetta had somehow gained entrance—"

I folded my arms. "How come I can see everything in the dark?"

His face fell. "I tried to tell you."

My mouth dropped open before I could stop it. "Tell me what? That you lied?" My mind tried to go over every detail of what had just occurred. I didn't remember drinking his blood. Had he wiped the experience from my thoughts?

"I bit my tongue, by accident."

"What?"

He stuck his tongue out at me. I raised my brows. He pulled his tongue back in. "My cell phone vibrated just as I was kissing you, and I bit my tongue in surprise. When I kissed you deeply, I had no idea I had cut my tongue and drawn blood."

"You shared your blood with me? You said—"

"I meant what I said. I made a mistake. But—"

Betrayed by a deceiving vampire! I grabbed one of my heart-shaped velvet pillows and threw it at him, unable to curb my fury. "Get out!"

"If I go outside, Lynetta will be waiting for me."

My heart instantly stopped, and I swallowed convulsively. "I *meant*, out of my bedroom." Jeez, no way had I wanted him to be at the mercy of the sick vamp. The thought of throwing him outside and her bloody fangs ripping at his throat...I shuddered.

He looked so miserable that I reconsidered my actions and harsh words. But he had shared his blood with me, and now I could see in the dark like a vampire could. What else had he done to me with that one kiss?

"I don't think I could have changed you much more than that, Marissa, if it eases your mind any. You couldn't have had much of my blood."

My temperature was still elevated with irritation. He was supposed to give me a choice.

"I didn't do it on purpose. I swear it. I would never have done that to you without asking you to go along with it. If you want me to leave, I will." Though he was sincere, I sensed he hoped with all his heart I would not send him out to face the vamp.

The idea he would leave the house and be at Lynetta's mercy terrified me and bile rose in my throat. I shook my head. "Not the house. I don't want you to leave the safety of the house."

"I'm so sorry, Marissa. Truly, I am."

"All right." I tried to rein my anger in, realizing on some other level that he hadn't planned what had happened. "Somehow, we'll beat her," I tried to reassure him and myself.

He nodded, though he still looked terribly disconcerted.

"Goodnight."

He hesitated, seemingly wanting to comfort me, but I wasn't in the mood to tolerate his touch. He seemed to sense how I felt and left the room, shutting the door behind him.

I sat on my bed, wrapped my arms tightly around me, trying to comfort myself. Knowing I had been changed now, too, I wondered if he knew what he was talking about. Had he transferred other strange abilities to me that I was still unaware of?

One thing I couldn't do was read his mind. Maybe he was right, then. Perhaps the only thing that had changed about me was my ability to see in the dark. That certainly wasn't a bad thing. Could save on electricity. Would help when I drove at night.

I crawled under my covers and hugged them underneath my chin. Still the notion nagged at me...what had we truly done?

"Know this, sweet Marissa. I truly love you with all my heart."

I stared at the wall that hid him from my view. He hadn't spoken a word...not out loud. I could read his mind?

"Dominic!"

6

T HE DREAMS

FURIOUS WITH DOMINIC, but unable to stay awake any longer to hold the grudge, my eyes closed and my world collided, shifted and collapsed. In its place, I saw a new world, time past, alien, fleeting glimpses—totally weird.

Through Dominic's eyes, I saw visions of the past and like an outsider looking in, I watched history reveal itself—at least a fraction of Dominic's history.

A slightly older version of Dominic, his hair as dark but spiked, his eyes more hazel, his lips thinned in a scowl. "How many times do I have to tell you, Dominic? Don't mess with witches!"

"Hey, James, she smiled at me. She's interested."

He was wrong. I knew he was wrong.

James shook his head. "She was smiling at a warlock eating a burger across the restaurant. Not at you."

Yes, listen to James. He's right.

Dominic slapped his brother on the shoulder. "Says you. Just watch this."

Every nerve taut, I could see where this was leading, but I was unable to stop the forward motion.

The three witches sat at a yellow table. The redhead, Carissa Merriweather, swirled a French fry in a blob of ketchup, the brunette, Linnie Armstrong, licked the mustard off a hamburger, coating her tongue yellow, and the blonde, Little Miss Perfect Debbie Damint— the one that had stolen Dominic's interest—flipped her hair back, then took a bite of a chicken sandwich.

I have to back away. None of these girls will put up with an annoying human boy. But I was moving like a train without brakes into the path of an unyielding girl—with unknown powers—and I was sure I would dearly suffer the consequences.

"Hey," Dominic said to Debbie. Her blue eyes sparkled in the fluorescent lights, and he thought she was the most beautiful girl he'd seen in a long time. Especially when she smiled at him.

But as soon as he opened his mouth to speak further, the witch stood, her face turning hard. "What do you want?" Her words and eyes were icy.

I'd never seen her react so vehemently, but then again, she put the charms on warlocks and not humans. Immediately, I wanted to move out of her way before she did anything nasty. I wanted to, but I was frozen to the tile floor.

Dominic should have taken the cue. He should have listened to his brother, but he was certain she had smiled at him, not at some warlock. "Would you like to go to a movie with me later tonight?"

"Get lost," she snarled.

Yes, get lost. Good advice. And if I could, I would heed it.

Dominic wasn't buying it. As far as he was concerned the witch didn't mean it. The other girls laughed, and he knew it was because of them that she'd changed her attitude.

He was wrong. If I didn't back off, something bad was going to happen.

"Turn him into a toad," Carissa said, her green eyes narrowed.

"Yeah, a warty, slimy thing," Linnie, the parrot of the three, agreed, nodding her head, then taking another sip of her soda.

I hoped and prayed the witches weren't any good at spells. Debbie wasn't in any of my classes except P.E., though I'd heard she was a whiz at potions. I had no idea about the other girls and their spell-casting abilities.

Dominic smiled. The blue-eyed blonde would not do such a dastardly thing.

I knew better. The look in Debbie's chilly eyes, the way her lips began to move silently. I tried to counteract the spell, but I didn't succeed. The spell worked its way through every molecule of my body, the shrinking and changing of cells. My heart rate changed from beating like a scared rabbit's to something much smaller.

In a heartbeat, Dominic found himself looking up from the floor, his voice croaking, his skin covered in olive drab bumps and definitely slimy. The witches laughed.

"Oh, God," I squeaked out. Everyone had turned into giants, towering over me, staring at me. The girls wore hideous grins, their eyes black with humor, while James looked like he was ready to be sick. I felt incredibly flat, as my round, fat body hugged the floor. Worse, a fly flitting about caught my attention and I had the worst urge to zap him with my tongue. *Ewww.*

James pleaded with Debbie. "You've taught him a lesson. Please turn him back."

"Nah," Carissa said, twirling a red curl around her fingers. "Leave him like that at least overnight."

A girl screamed when she saw Dominic. The scrawny manager, who appeared to be a college student trying to earn some extra money, wiped his greasy hands on a dishtowel and hurried over. His brow furrowed and he motioned to Dominic. "Take the frog out of here."

"Toad," Carissa said, sneering. "Frogs can turn into handsome princes. Toads are only meant to be one thing—mud-dwelling toads."

"Please, I promise I'll take him home with me and that's the last you'll see of him," James said.

Please, listen to James.

Debbie's lips curved up. Dominic knew she'd change him back.

I knew she wouldn't.

But Dominic thought she'd only turned him in the first place because of her friends.

I knew it wasn't true.

For half an hour, the manager insisted they take him outside, James pleaded with the witch, and Dominic craved a mud bath for his itchy, dry skin.

And I couldn't wait to get out of the nightmare as another fly buzzed nearby and I was losing control of my hunger pangs.

Then an older witch and her kids entered the restaurant and as soon as she did, Debbie and the other girls looked concerned.

Yeah, using magic on humans for a witch's or warlock's amusement wasn't allowed. And if I could, I would teach Debbie some spells of my own, if I could remember them.

Debbie quickly wiggled her fingers in the air and said some incantation under her breath.

Instantly, I felt release. I was nearly eye level with James again, my skin nice and smooth, my voice back to normal.

Before Dominic could speak, James yanked him outside. "Of all the harebrained schemes of yours. I can't believe you pulled this."

"Don't tell Mom and Dad, okay?"

I had the sinking feeling he might. Please, please don't tell them about this. I figured they would ground me for a good month.

James shook his head.

Kids laughing at an outdoor table, the spicy aroma of grilled burgers drifting from the restaurant, the feel of the hot air pressing against me faded into nothingness.

Then as if the lights in a theater were suddenly turned on and the play was about to begin again, I found myself back inside the burger place, different cars parked out front, a different scrawny college-age manager and a girl who looked like real trouble.

Lynetta batted her long black eyelashes as soon as she spied Dominic at the Hamburger Spot. Her enticing smile was perfectly genuine. And when she pointed her finger at him and crooked it, motioning to him to join her, he knew she was a dream come true.

But I tried to warn him—she's a vampire! Don't get near her!

Though usually he liked blue-eyed blondes, this girl's hair and eyes were as black as shiny onyx—fathomless.

He seemed to glide across the crowded burger hangout to join her.

No, not the burger place. We were suddenly in the darkened alley across the street, the smell of wet asphalt from a recent shower and of garbage cooking in an overstuffed garbage dumpster wafting in the air. How in the world did we get here?

For a moment, I felt disoriented, my stomach swirling with a strange sensation, like I'd been spinning around in a Mad Hatter tea cup and it had suddenly stopped.

Lynetta tugged Dominic into her arms and began kissing him like there was no tomorrow.

No tomorrow. No...no, there will be no tomorrow if you let her do this!

All at once the noxious odors disappeared. Nothing existed but the woman pressing her body nice and close. Her full lips tasted like forbidden fruit—a sweet wine. The alcoholic content nearly made him swoon with headiness.

No, no, not the wine. The woman. The vamp!

She licked his lips, teasing them apart, then tangled her tongue with his. He groaned.

I could have kicked him. Break free from the vamp's spell! She's old! Way…way too old for you. And really bad news.

Her hands held his face still, his eyes closed, he was in love.

Idiot!

And then her teeth grazed his neck. The prelude to the bite.

Break free! I so don't want to feel this. I tried to break away.

Her lips caressed his throat and he was barely able to stand when she bit him. Hard.

The pain, the syringe-like stabs, the burning sensation, I wanted to collapse. My knees weakened. My senses reeled. I felt like I was falling from a space capsule, kick-dropped into the black void.

Her blood was on his lips, his tongue and down his throat. And then all he recalled was being alone in a dark alley, no sign of the girl, his mind drifting, his skin pale, and strange images were flashing before his eyes.

I didn't want to see what happened next, my stomach tightening, my fists forming under my pillow, but I was powerless to stop it.

Dominic closed his eyes, trying to block out the strange images floating across his tired brain, but couldn't. He leaned against the brick wall in the dark alley, his stomach swimming.

I wanted to leave, return home, safe, away from the world I'd found myself in. But I was far, far from home in a different time and place.

The plague had hit England hard and thousands in the city had died. Even the crown prince had taken ill, but just when Lynetta thought she wouldn't take another breath, something happened. Weak from starvation, she could barely move, but her throat burned as if it were on fire, and she craved blood worse than she'd ever wanted anything before. Everyone in her family—her mother, father, aunts

*and two sisters—had already died, their bodies burned with the rest of
the plague victims, their house condemned.*

The smells here were even worse than in the alley where I'd
just been.

*A candle no longer lit the room late that night, yet Lynetta could
see as if the room was illuminated by burning tallow. The sound of a
rat scurrying across the floor in the dark caught her attention, and she
could even hear its heart beating. Every muscle stiff and unresponsive,
she rolled off the straw mattress and headed for the rat.*

Panic filled me. No, no. Rats carry the plague. Don't touch
the rat!

*With a monumental effort, Lynetta dove for the rodent. But
instead of crashing into the table where the rat ducked for safety, she
half glided, half flew.*

The sensation made me feel like I had grown wings, my
body weightless and unencumbered. For an instant, I forgot
about the rat. But then the gnawing in my belly grew.

*Lynetta didn't think she would make it in time to reach the scur-
rying rodent. And she really wasn't sure what she would do with the
filthy creature if she caught it. But in the next instant, she held it in
her hands, bit off its head and was drinking its warm blood. And
loving every drop of it.*

I shuddered, unable to get the image of fur and blood out of
my brain or the taste of the vermin out of my mouth. Raw, filthy
blood, yet the taste of it warm against my tongue settled the
craving.

*"Famished?" a man asked, peering into Lynetta's room. "My name
is Count William Dubois, at your service." He made a sweeping bow
as if she was the queen of England.*

I stared at him. My God. He looked like...like Dominic.

*Dark-haired and eyed, the man stood six feet tall, his skin pale, his
lips stained with blood and lifted upward in a sensuous smile.*

"Lynetta Tolliver," she said, stretching out her hand. He vanished

and reappeared before her, reached for her hand, and kissed it with great finesse.

I nearly swooned.

Lynetta nearly did, too, but she didn't think it was because of the gentleman's gallantness, but because she was so ill and still starving.

Images of his being with her throughout the centuries passed before my eyes in a series of flickering video clips. Then I watched as another vampire ripped out William's throat and Lynetta killed her lover's murderer. It all happened so quickly, it was mostly a blur.

Dangerous and feral, she wanted someone else, someone to replace William, and she began stalking the streets for her new lover.

Spying Dominic Vorchowsky at the teen hangout, she waved her finger at him, drawing him forth, her gaze locked onto his, seducing him, willing him, commanding him. He would replace her lost love for all eternity.

And he couldn't resist her allure.

I wanted to scream at the vamp, wanted to fight for Dominic, for his soul, for his life back and I kicked my covers aside, but couldn't fully wake from the dreams.

Then I settled into a deep sleep where darkness ruled.

I waited for Marissa to scream out my name again, but when she didn't, I knew she just needed her sleep. As did I. At least I hoped she would be more reasonable when the day dawned.

I squirmed in bed, knowing that by sharing Marissa's blood, I was destined to visit her dreams, her memories, her past. Just like when Lynetta had taken my blood. I still couldn't believe how much I looked like Count William Dubois. I could have been William's reincarnation. Though I wasn't. Other than glimpses from Lynetta's memories, I didn't know anything about the man.

My mind drifted and my thoughts shifted to a witch's world —Marissa's.

I wasn't sure where I was. A theater, filled with students. I glanced at the stage. A flag embossed with beakers sat on the stage to the right. And a gray-haired old woman motioned to a kid. "Your turn, Debbie Damint."

"Did you ever figure out what your spell project would be?" Kate asked Marissa.

She smiled. "Absolutely."

"You've been fretting about it all semester and never said a word. So give. What did you come up with?"

"You'll see."

Everyone in the spells class took their seats in the auditorium, and then one by one the students showed off their spells, starting with the average classes. Kate conjured up an imaginary dragon which was so real, her teacher threatened to move her to the advanced class—again. But she would never apply herself in class.

Remnants of dragon smoke drifted off the stage and the teacher motioned for Marissa to show off her spell next. With a spring to her step, she walked on stage. Some of the students were sleeping, some talking to each other, very few were paying attention. But she would get their attention—guaranteed.

She raised her hands and began the incantation. After repeating it for the third time, a swirl of blue water whirled around the floor until the water formed into the figure of a woman.

Her aquamarine eyes large and expressive, her full lips turned up in a slight smile, her hair draping down her slim hips, blending in with her watery cerulean blue gown, ribbons of cobalt contrasting with the lighter blues—she was one of the most interesting creatures I'd ever seen.

The woman epitomized beauty. Sure, Kate's dragon was

pretty cool. But this was beyond extraordinary. An A+ project for sure.

Certainly, she had everyone's attention. A woman was waving her hand at the stage and Marissa's teacher was nodding. The teacher hurried up the stairs to the stage but kept her distance from the water figure. "That is not a proper spell, Marissa Lakeland. Do you have a real one prepared for class?"

I felt horrible. Why wasn't the spell acceptable? I'd never seen anything like it. Not anything the other students had conjured up came close to this.

"I…I can cast a cupid's arrow spell."

Her teacher frowned. "You need willing participants ahead of time. Take your seat."

The creature stood nearby, her watery skin and clothes shimmering in the bright lights, watching the students.

"But my grade…"

"Zero. You cannot…" The gray-haired woman motioned to the entity. "This doesn't count."

A zero. I glowered at the teacher. How could she be so unfair? The water creature was the best spell ever.

Marissa waved her hand at her creation and spoke under her breath, then took her seat next to Kate. Tears ran down her cheeks. Trying to console her, Kate patted her hand. "I could have told you bringing her here wouldn't have been acceptable."

Fuming, I clenched my teeth. If I'd been the teacher, Marissa would have received an A+ and extra credit, too.

A puddle of water sat on the stage where the water creature had been. The next four students slipped on the wet floor, and the teacher, scowling the whole time, stopped the proceedings until she could get a janitor to mop up the floor.

The stage and the students, the teacher and the theater shifted, darkened, vanished.

I opened my eyes and listened for the sound of Marissa stirring, but I sensed her mind was finally cloaked in deep sleep, thank the stars.

If Marissa had been sucked into the dream swap while she slept, I sincerely hoped she hadn't seen Lynetta kissing me, or how much I'd enjoyed it. I groaned and ran my fingers through my hair. I had a sneaking suspicion she would be ticked off at me in the morning.

7

D OMINIC

EARLY THE NEXT MORNING, I entered the kitchen. No sign of Marissa yet, though I'd heard her clunking around in the bathroom, so she was probably doing whatever girls do to make themselves presentable. *Poor things.* It didn't take any time at all for us guys to rejoin the world and still be our handsome selves. Though it helped that I no longer had to shave, which was a remarkable vampiric trait I totally agreed with.

I, the Prince of Darkness, had been certain the love of my life who called out my name with such hostility before she fell asleep truly didn't wish to see me. Hopefully, the dreams she'd seen were not too disturbing. If Marissa enjoyed a good night's sleep, she would be more reasonable. Then she would see how her new abilities could benefit her. How many other witches did she know that could do the things, whatever they might be, that she could?

Seeing in the dark was one of the most remarkable feats I enjoyed. I hoped if I was saved from being turned fully, that I might still keep some of the more admirable traits...like seeing my lovely soul mate without any kind of light, natural or otherwise. The cursed desire for blood, my skin's aversion to the sun's rays, and my fangs extending when angered or hungry for blood —I would thankfully do without.

I glanced out the three big windows where a light oak breakfast table sat to see what kind of day we were in for. To the north, a dark blue wall headed in our direction, thunder grumbling in the distance around Dallas, and sparks of lightning flared to light up the darkness. A thick blanket of clouds hung high overhead—another spring storm was headed our way. No sun to bother my sensitive skin. Good, I could go to school with Marissa.

Marissa stalked into the kitchen dressed in black jeans and a black T-shirt with a red universal hazard symbol embossed on it and beneath this in bright red letters, *Boy Hazard* was written. My lips twitched with amusement. She definitely was. A light floral fragrance she wore wafted in the air, triggering my need to lift my nose and take my fill. Another great attribute at times, my sense of smell had vastly improved. The downside was being able to smell offensive odors better, too. But Marissa's appearance instantly brought to mind the notion of having a good morning kiss.

She glanced in my direction, scowled, and quickly turned away. I was sure she wasn't thinking of good morning kisses. Dark circles appeared beneath her clear blue eyes. The low rounded neck of her shirt exposed the two tiny bite marks, but they were barely visible. Only a small bit of yellow bruising marred the area.

Instantly, the human part of me regretted even so much as causing her the slightest bit of discomfort. The vampire side of me couldn't help but feel I'd claimed my soul mate for all eternity. She was mine now, and I even felt more possessive of her than I had when I first caught sight of her, if that was possible. Even last night, if some guy had made a pass at Marissa at the burger place, I would have been hard put to keep my fangs intact.

My mother had always said it was the same way for her and Dad, well, minus the fangs, when they had first met—love at first sight. Of course, I never believed in such a thing, not until I saw my lifemate. I wondered if I hadn't been changed, how different it would have been for us? How would I have encouraged our relationship if I hadn't needed her help so badly?

Marissa whipped around and yanked a milk jug from the fridge. She wouldn't acknowledge I existed. She was still pissed, but that wouldn't stop me from trying to get into her good graces.

When my dad was in one of his states of depression—usually over the stresses at work because he had one of those overbearing bosses who micromanaged everything—I found humor often helped to lighten his mood. Sitting down at the kitchen bar, I rested my elbows on the white tile countertop and took on a leisurely posture, as if I joined her every morning for breakfast after having slept the night beside her—beyond her bedroom wall.

"I'll have a cheese omelet with a side order of hash browns and sausage. But if you don't have sausage, bacon will do. And two slices of toast, coated with blackberry jam. Or honey. No, make it blackberry. If you have it."

She glanced at me, her blue eyes ice daggers. Now I had her attention. I truly didn't expect her to become a short-order cook. I only wanted her to say something to me, though I figured she would give me a nasty earful. Still, anything was better than bitter silence between us.

"I'm sorry that you can't stand the bitter silence between us. But you shouldn't have—"

This time it was my turn to be surprised. Now the shoe was on the other foot...my foot. She'd read my mind, and I hadn't expected that at all.

"Yeah, Prince of Darkness. I can read your mind." She tapped a spoon on the counter. "And I'm so glad you don't expect me to cook that huge breakfast you just ordered. But if you fix it for yourself, remember to clean up. I'm not your housemaid either."

Figuring it would make her madder, I attempted not to smile, but I couldn't help myself. After getting over the initial shock that she could read my mind, which definitely was going to be a switch—I mean, when I read her mind, it seemed...*my right*, but now that she could read my private thoughts...I shook my head. In any event, I couldn't help smiling at her snappy but cute response.

She ignored me, gulped her glass of milk, then grabbed a black canvas book bag. "I'll be home at noon."

My heart thundering, I jumped off the leather barstool. No way would I let her out of my sight now. "I'm going with you."

She swung around, glaring at me, her voice rising an octave. "What?"

"Listen, I'm going to stick by you from now on." I didn't want to scare her, but I truly feared losing her.

Now her tone changed, her eyes wide with disbelief, or maybe concern. "Lynetta can't run around in the daylight, can she?"

"No, but she has human hosts she feeds off. She could have any one of them come for you and take you to her lair after what you did to protect me last night."

Marissa stared at the counter for a moment as if considering the notion, then turned to me. "They'll never let you into the school. You have to be a warlock. Know any spells you can cast?"

I would not be thwarted no matter what. "No, but maybe you could teach me a few on the way over to school."

She shook her head. "You have to be a warlock to have the ability. Mere humans can't work our spells."

"But I'm not a mere human anymore." In fact, several of the feats I could perform now were quite remarkable.

Lifting her bag off her shoulder, Marissa set it on the counter. "Can you levitate my book bag?"

She had me there. "I can vanish and reappear as mist."

"Won't help. Warlocks can't do things like that. They would know something was wrong with you."

That hurt.

She hurried for the front door.

I reappeared before her. Running into my chest, she let out a small cry of surprise. I grabbed her arms to steady her, still wanting that good-morning kiss. Touching her sent warmth spiraling through me that couldn't be denied. "Sorry, Marissa, I can't let you go to school without me."

Through clenched teeth, she reluctantly agreed. "All right. But don't say I didn't warn you. If they poke and prod you and put you on display, it won't be my doing."

"You left out the stripped…"

She glanced down at my red T-shirt and blue jeans. Her lips curved up just a bit, but somehow, she managed to hide from me the mental images that I'm sure flitted across her brain. "Yeah, well, it won't be my fault if the schoolmaster tries to expose you for what you are. But where did you get the change of clothes?"

"I popped back to my parents' home and took the clothes from the closet."

"Neat trick. Did you visit with them?"

"My mother gets upset every time she sees me. Besides, everyone was still sleeping."

A flicker of concern shone in Marissa's expressive eyes, but then the look faded and she pulled her front door open.

Kate stood with her hand on the doorbell. She stared blankly and her mouth opened when she saw me with Marissa. Her green eyes couldn't grow any bigger.

Marissa's eyes widened as much.

Trying to remedy the situation, I quickly stepped outside and offered my hand to Kate. "New kid at the school. I asked Marissa if she would show me the way."

Ignoring my outstretched hand, Kate turned her attention to Marissa and waited for an explanation.

"Yeah, he, uh, just asked if I could show him the way."

"I just said that, Marissa. Quit acting so nervous. She'll suspect something's wrong," I telepathically communicated to her.

Marissa glared at me.

"Here let me take your book bag," I offered belatedly to Marissa. One thing about being a vampire, my muscles were much stronger. I could lift nearly twice my own weight, without ever exercising a bit.

"I'm fine," she said, her words couched in irritation.

"You can carry *my* bag." Kate stretched the blue canvas pack out to me.

Reluctantly, I took Kate's bag and slung it over my shoulder. Again, I tried to smooth out the difficulty Marissa and I were having. "Marissa?"

"No!"

"You can't be mad at me forever."

Then again, maybe she could. I didn't know much about her. Maybe she was the kind of girl that held lifelong grudges.

"No, normally I don't hold grudges. But with you I'm bound to make an exception."

Kate studied me way too closely, and I assumed she realized I was the Prince of Darkness she had chased so fervently last night. When her eyes caught sight of the puncture marks on Marissa's neck, she shifted her attention back to me way too rapidly. She was quickly putting one and one together and coming up with conclusions that could get me into really hot water. On the other hand, I wasn't going to let Marissa go it alone. Not when Lynetta would most likely attempt to get back at her.

Reading my mind, Marissa handed me her bag. Thank God for thinking the right thoughts.

Marissa said, "This is Thomas Reading, Kate. And Thomas, this is Kate Witherspoon. Sorry I forgot to make introductions." She slowed her step along the sidewalk.

"Thomas Reading?" I cleared my throat, exasperated. *"She already knows the Prince of Darkness's name was Dominic Vor... something or other ending with a 'ski'."*

Marissa glared at me while Kate cast a look from me to Marissa, knowing the truth, kind of.

"She knows, Marissa, that I'm the guy from the Hamburger Spot. And since you told her that my name was Dominic Vorchowsky, I think it best to leave it at that. Besides, I'll have a devil of a time remembering some other name. I'm not a trained secret agent man."

Marissa huffed her displeasure. "I meant to say this is Dominic Vorchowsky."

Kate's lips parted, her green eyes darkened, but she didn't speak.

"You know, the guy we saw at the Hamburger Spot. He was pretty amused you—well, *we*—thought he was a vampire."

"You told him?" Her voice etched in surprise, Kate looked back at the bite marks.

"Yeah. When you walked into your house last night, he

hurried to catch up to me. Said he was going to our same school and wondered if he could walk with me...*us*, this morning."

"He lives around here?" This time Kate's words were elevated and sounded panicky.

"Yes," I said in my most charming manner, trying to show I wasn't anything evil.

Kate stared at me, then looked down at the sidewalk while we continued to stroll to school.

"Yes, can you imagine how silly it was of us to think he was a vampire? Why look at how he's out here with us in broad daylight."

Kate again looked at me, as if wondering whether I could just disintegrate any moment. Gladdened that Marissa could think of something brilliant to say to dispel her girlfriend's worry, I smiled.

Marissa offered me an arresting smile. *"Brilliant, huh?"*

"Yeah, and you'd better believe I'll take you to the school dance." Though I couldn't quash the concern that she would be disappointed in my lack of dancing skills.

She raised her brows, then slipped her hand around mine. *"But you can't."*

I lifted my chin. *"I'll find a way."* If nothing else, I would be there to ensure no warlocks laid a hand on my girl.

She rubbed her temple, a frown marring her hopeful expression. *"Forget it. I wouldn't want you to get into trouble."*

"Nah, we'll think of something." I was certain if we put our heads together, we could come up with some kind of a plan. Surely one of my princely gifts could be used to mimic a warlock's abilities.

Kate studied me, then turned to Marissa. Her gaze locked onto our clasped hands. She looked back at Marissa. Even though I couldn't read her thoughts, I could pretty well guess what was going on in her mind. She still wondered if I were a vampire and somehow was exercising control over Marissa. But she couldn't figure out how I could survive during the daylight hours.

Marissa, reading my thoughts, added, "Oh, yes, and Dominic loves the burgers at the Hamburger Spot, too. His favorite place to hang out."

Kate looked back at me.

"Another winning argument, Marissa. Thanks for saving my butt."

She glanced behind me. *"From what I can tell, it's a butt worth saving."*

My smile stretched across my face in triumph. She was my girl again.

She squeezed my hand, and I grimaced. Her strength had significantly increased, and my eyes watered. Quickly loosening her hold, she frowned at me.

She was back to being mad at me again.

"But just think of it this way, Marissa, we can fight Lynetta easier if you have vampire strength."

Marissa muttered something unintelligible.

"You don't have a book bag, Dominic," Kate said, her words a definite challenge to my story. "Are you prepared for school?"

The question was loaded. I didn't have a scrap of paper to take notes, nor a pen or pencil to write with. It did seem a little odd that I wouldn't have something to take to school.

"They haven't even unpacked all of their household goods, and Dominic's book bag is still packed away somewhere in one of the boxes. He can borrow one of my notepads for the day," Marissa quickly suggested.

I took a ragged breath. I hadn't expected Marissa's girlfriend to pose such a threat to me. Still, if we could master her, we could make it through a day of school, I thought.

"But what if I don't have any of the same classes as you? Really,

Dominic, I think this is a bad idea. Maybe if you just walk me to school, and then return for me after classes end, you can escort me safely home. Wouldn't that be a better idea?"

There was no way I was letting her go through a day of classes unprotected. She had no idea how vengeful Lynetta could be. *"No. Well, I mean, it might have been a good idea except for a couple of things. Number one, it's not the plan we spoke to Kate about. And secondly, I'm afraid Lynetta might send her minions after you. We have to put on as good a show as we can."*

Marissa swallowed hard as we came into view of the rambling white brick buildings attached by covered walkways. Blue roofs topped with flags identified each of the classrooms, and I tried to imagine what they stood for.

Marissa shared her thoughts on which buildings housed which classrooms: *"A white-haired and bearded warlock on black for the spells room, a white-haired witch on purple for the potions room, a castle for the history of witchcraft, a fairy godmother-type woman featured on the flag for manners..."*

I grinned at Marissa, amused the school would teach manners to witches and warlocks. She poked me in the ribs.

Then a new concern popped into my head. What if the witch who had turned me into a toad was at this school? She had to have the worst manners of any of the students.

Marissa gave me a sinister glare, and I realized at once she had seen my folly in a dream. Did she know the girl?

"Absolutely. Debbie Damint. All the guys fall all over themselves for her. So you'd better not ask her out to the movies again, or face the consequences."

So I was really in the doghouse now.

Marissa nodded. "I'll take Dominic to the main building to register him," she said to Kate.

"I have no plan to speak to this Debbie Damint, Marissa. It was just a really bad mistake."

"Right."

Then a new worry consumed me. What if I ran into her or any of her girlfriends who were with her at the Hamburger Spot? She would recognize I had been a human and then what?

Marissa shook her head. *"Wouldn't you know I would have to get mixed up with a…a Prince of Darkness who had the hots for Debbie Damint?"*

"Sorry, Marissa. It won't happen again. I swear it! She was just a distraction before I met you—the real thing."

"Stop, before you dig yourself any deeper."

"Are we still on for lunch afterwards?" Kate asked Marissa, her look hopeful, yet I sensed she wanted to get Marissa off to herself in private and interrogate her thoroughly.

"Uhm, I think—"

"We would love it," I broke in, hoping to not raise Kate's ire or suspicion any further.

Marissa frowned at me. *"The more Kate sees us together, the more suspicious she'll be, Dominic!"*

"If you don't do the things you normally do with her, she'll become even more suspicious."

"Marissa?" Kate asked, encouraging her to agree.

"Yes, of course, Kate, as always. If you don't mind Dominic tagging along."

"Not at all. Since he's so new and doesn't have any friends." Kate said the words sarcastically, as if she didn't believe I was new to the area in the least.

"Right."

I handed Kate's bag to her. She thanked me but looked back at Marissa's neck. I knew before long she'd question her about it.

Marissa dropped my hand when we walked into the administration building. A plump woman with white hair piled on top of her head and piercing blue eyes studied me. She instantly made me think of the grandmotherly-looking movie versions of Mrs. Santa Claus, except for the harsh eyes.

"This is Dominic Vorchowsky, Mrs. Remington. He just moved here and needs to be registered."

"Your old school records?" she asked, putting me on the spot immediately.

"I've come from Germany, Mrs. Remington. I'm afraid it might take a while to get the records. But I didn't want to lose any more schooling."

She raised a white brow. "Interesting. You have no German accent." She glanced at Marissa and dismissed her. "You may go to class."

Quickly, Marissa jumped in to rescue me. "Can you assign him to my classes? I can show him around and—"

"We'll have to test Mr. Vorchowsky first. We have no idea what level he'll be in."

"Test him?" Marissa squeaked.

I could sense the terror in Marissa's thoughts. I rested my hand on her shoulder to reassure her. "If I don't do well, it may be because my education is lacking. However, I will try my utmost to succeed." The notion came to mind again that I was unable to control a witch's thoughts. It would have been so very simple to compel Mrs. Remington to allow me to stay with Marissa the rest of the day and to forgo the test if she'd been human.

"Very well. At least you have a good attitude, young man, more than I can say about some of the warlocks who attend the school." Mrs. Remington motioned to Marissa to leave.

Marissa's eyes grew misty as she looked back at me, her heart thundering. I could hear the blood rushing through her veins, panicked.

"I'll be all right, truly, dear Marissa. Go to class."

"You won't know how to do any spells. She'll prove you're a fraud."

"She thinks I've come from a foreign country. Maybe she'll allow me some mistakes."

Marissa shook her head, knowing the school administrator would soon prove me an impostor. Then she headed out of the building.

Feeling horrible that I couldn't reassure her, I realized I couldn't even reassure myself this would work. Instead, I envisioned Mrs. Remington calling the head of security and having him or her toss me out on my ear.

"All right, Mr. Vorchowsky. Now we'll see what you've learned in your old school. We'll start with something fairly simple. Levitate my pen holder, will you?"

Having hoped my vampire abilities would help slip me through the tests, I gulped at her suggestion.

Levitation?

8

M ARISSA

BULLHEADED, that's what Dominic was.

I couldn't help being terrified that he would be in trouble, though. Chill bumps covered my arms and legs, and I could barely breathe.

Did he think he could sneak into a witches' and warlocks' school without being a bona fide warlock? Nuts. He was absolutely nuts.

Not to mention if Debbie Damint caught sight of him, then what? She would remember him for sure, or one of the two witches she'd been with would. Linnie, the brunette, and Carissa, the redhead, both meaner than fire ants on the attack.

Still, I had to protect him, since he thought I was Marissa, his savior. Even though I was still perturbed with him for turning me into a...well, a Princess of Darkness. Though in part, some of my new abilities were kind of funky.

I stood at the administration window and chanced peeking in. I read poor Dominic's thoughts. Mrs. Remington had her back to me, and Dominic was concentrating on levitating the pen container on her desk. Just when I began to cast a spell on the container, the desk lifted. Then the chair and the pen container.

Mrs. Remington quickly waved her arms around, and all of the items settled back down with a thud.

I dropped my mouth wide open. *How in the world...*

Mrs. Remington pointed to a drawing board. *Now what?*

Dominic concentrated on the board. He was to write the ingredients and potion for making a body invisible. He smiled. But I did not. He could make himself invisible, sure, but not the way a warlock would.

I jammed my hand into my bag, then yanked my potion book out. Flipping through the pages, I hurriedly searched for the correct potion that I could never remember by heart even if my life—or in this case Dominic's—depended on it. I would transfer the directions for the potion via my thoughts. He knew I was outside the window, but he tried to concentrate on the administrator's words, not the thoughts I tried to convey to him.

Pay attention! I wanted to yell at him.

Before I had the correct page, he began to write the ingredients. I looked down at my book, then back at the board. He had correctly listed every one of them. *How did he do that?*

"*Seems you transferred some of your skills to me, dear Marissa.*"

"*Dominic?*"

He turned toward the window and gave me a satisfied smile. "*Seems I'm a bona fide warlock now.*"

"*But...but I never could remember this potion.*"

"*I always excelled at chemistry. Seems you have the thoughts in your subconscious but can never use them when you need them. But they're there. Somehow, you transferred them to me. Though I really thought I was sunk with that levitation spell."*

My head spun with the notion. What else would we learn he could do, or I could do because of the blood transference? Then another worry took hold. *"Now she'll put you in the advanced classes. I'm only average."*

"You'll never be average to me, Marissa."

Loving how he said the right words, I smiled.

"Marissa, what are you doing here?" a deep male voice asked, belonging to Joshua Cantaleaver, the cutest warlock in school until Dominic slipped into my life.

My heart leapt in my throat and my skin grew clammy as I whirled around to see Joshua studying me. Dressed in dress slacks and a preppy sweater, he always looked like he was going to hobnob with the Princes of England. I looked back through the window at Dominic. The look on his face had turned stormy. Instantly, I worried he would extend his fangs.

"On my way to class," I said to Joshua, hurriedly shoving my potions book into my bag.

"Want me to carry it for you?" He held out his hand.

What had gotten into him? He'd never shown any interest in me. Not in the ten years I'd been at the school. Not once.

Dominic appeared behind him. Just poof, and he was there. I frowned at him. *"Walk places, Dominic, before you get found out."*

"I had to get here sooner to protect my girl. Besides, I'm registered for school now. I'll walk you to our class."

I motioned to Dominic still standing behind Joshua. "My new friend—"

"Boyfriend," Dominic corrected with authority.

Joshua stared at Dominic, his black eyes heated. "Who are you?"

"I just told you. Dominic Vorchowsky, Marissa's steady."

"She doesn't have a steady." Joshua acted like if he said so, that was good enough for all of us, then turned to me and said, "I wanted to take you to the dance on Friday. I'll drop by your house at five."

My mouth gaped wide again. Had one of the students slipped him a love potion to play a trick on me—the most undated girl in school? Any such potion wouldn't last for long and by the time of the dance, it would have worn off, as well as Joshua's interest in me.

Dominic clenched his teeth and shook his head at Joshua. "I believe you didn't hear me right. Marissa will be my date Friday night and for every time in between and forever thereafter."

This time Joshua's mouth dropped, but then a hint of malice burned in his black eyes, though he didn't say a word to refute Dominic's claim.

Dominic grabbed my bag and slipped his hand over mine, then clutched it possessively. "Mrs. Remington said I had all of your classes."

"Witches' sports, too?" Joshua asked, his voice lilting upward, mocking Dominic.

"Spectator sports. I'm sure I'll enjoy that class the best."

Joshua folded his arms. "I'll see you in warlocks' gym. One on one."

I held Dominic's hand securely as Joshua took off for the history building. *"I have no idea why he has taken an interest in me all of a sudden. He has never—"*

"I know. I wonder if it's your friend, Kate, has put him up to it." Dominic motioned with his head to the spells building. Sure enough, Kate watched us through the window. *"I believe she might have bribed him to take an interest in you, to get you away from me, you know—worried for your safety."*

"Bribed him?" My brows lifted in annoyance.

"Well, I can't imagine anyone needing to be bribed to get inter-

ested in you, but if he has not been attracted to you before this, I would be highly suspicious of his motives now."

"*I am.*" But if Kate bribed Joshua... I growled inwardly, then a new thought bugged me. "How did you manage to get into my average classes? With all you did, I would think you would be assigned to the advanced classes."

"I was. But the administrator won't know which I'm actually attending for a while."

"You sure are cute. A bad boy, but awfully cute. Did you do things like this when you were just a human?"

His dark eyes sparkled with mischief. "You probably ought to get to know me a little better before I tell you all of my secrets."

I laughed. In the past, I'd always stayed away from bad-boy types. Now one was my steady? What next? "I knew you were too good to be true."

"Even if I'm a—"

I reached up and touched his lips. "My prince without his knight's armor."

He winked. "I believe you're the one rescuing me."

That notion tugged at my heartstrings. At least I hoped his faith in me was warranted.

Before we reached the spells building, I saw that sniping redheaded Carissa looking south and I hurried Dominic into the building before the witch noticed him.

Dominic glanced her way and his whole body tensed.

"She doesn't have spells class this period. And she's not in any of my other classes either."

Dominic relaxed. But we still hadn't even barely begun the day. If Linnie or Debbie Damint saw Dominic, I was sure we would be in for some trouble.

Dominic and I walked into the spells class where students stood talking with one another in groups of twos and threes, dressed like the typical blue jeans crowd, and none of them paying any attention to us. None but Kate, who folded her arms and studied us when we walked inside.

"Kate's mad at me."

Dominic nodded. *"For having a boyfriend who she believes to be a vampire."*

"And not telling her about it."

Her blond hair now moss green, Mrs. Robertson walked into the room. Last time her hair had turned that color, she'd said she'd gone swimming in the school's pool after hours and warned the girls who dyed their hair to wear caps in the pool. Guess she forgot her own advice. She motioned to the seats forming a half circle, three rows deep. Spell books of ancient and contemporary times lined shelves along two of the walls, a third of which I'd read, but retaining the information was my biggest problem. And large floor-to-ceiling windows looked out upon a grassy courtyard where some students ran on a track. I wished Dominic and I could be out there, right now, away from the watchful eyes of Kate and the teacher.

"Oh, my, we have a new student today," Mrs. Robertson cooed, as if she'd found a new victim to charm.

He raised his brows.

"She's fond of the male students in her classes. She barely tolerates us girls."

"Oh."

I couldn't tell if he thought that was a good thing or bad, which bugged me.

"And who might you be?" Mrs. Robertson shoved rimless glasses on her nose and squinted at a roster. "I don't have anyone new on my list."

"Dominic Vorchowsky, ma'am, just arrived this morning."

A grin split across her face. "So polite, too. All right, well, why don't you take a seat right there?" She pointed to a plastic chair close to where she stood.

Okay, that could be a bad thing.

I pulled an extra pad of paper and pen out of my book bag for Dominic, then joined Kate at our desks in the last row.

"I want to know everything!" Kate whispered harshly in my ear.

Mrs. Robertson rapped her wand on the podium. "Students, take your seats and let's begin our lessons."

Dominic passed along a telepathic message to me. *"So the inquisition begins."*

"Yes, but you don't have to be the one answering Kate's questions."

"Okay, class, today we're working on a spell to clear the mind. We can use this on humans, should one wish to harm us. The effect is only temporary. But if a human should approach me with a weapon, for example, I could make him forget what he wanted to do with it. Then I could easily relieve him of the weapon and leave. We can use this on ourselves, also, if we wish to wipe out a current anxiety. For example, if I worried about an illness in the family, but I needed to concentrate on a test, I could put the worry aside for a while, then focus on taking the exam. As you can see, it's a useful spell. Any questions?"

Kate raised her hand. I glanced at her, wondering what she was up to. She never asked questions, always keeping as low a profile as she could in class. It wasn't that she wasn't smart, she was over the top in most subjects, but she just didn't apply herself like she could to move up to the advanced level classes. Me? Well, I struggled hard to even get average grades.

"Anyone who could save me from an ancient vampire is clearly brilliant, Marissa."

I smiled at Dominic when he turned back to give me a grin. He almost always said the right words.

"Yes, Miss Kate?" the teacher asked.

"Would the mind spell work on vampires?"

Snickers filled the room.

I could have killed Kate on the spot, though we'd been best friends since kindergarten.

Kate folded her arms, and the teacher smiled. "We're not in a fantasy class, dear. But hypothetically, yes, if the vampire was human."

But I wasn't sure the teacher was right. How would she know what a vampire was capable of? "But how would we know?" I asked, then wondered if I'd gone mad for posing the question out loud. Of course, my only thought was if Dominic and I could use it on Lynetta, maybe we would stand a chance to destroy her. The teacher waited for more of an explanation of my question. "I mean, since vampires have never been proven to be real, how would we know if we could wipe their minds of their thoughts, even for an instant?"

"Bring one to class tomorrow and we can test our theory."

Several kids laughed, except, of course, for Kate, Dominic, and me.

I glanced at Kate who glowered at Dominic, giving him the evil eye. Had she bribed Joshua to ask me to the dance like Dominic suspected? She'd be dead meat.

Kate turned to me and frowned.

"If there are no further questions, we'll begin the spell. Oh, though I probably don't need to mention this to you, the spell will not work on witches or warlocks, except in the instance where you can use it on yourself. So if you want your mother to forget to serve calf's liver for supper, it won't work."

Several groaned at the mention of eating liver.

I wondered though, did Kate think she could cast the spell on Dominic? Or was it a way of her warning us that she knew he was a…Prince of Darkness?

"Once we memorize the spell, who will we get to test it on?" Kate asked.

"I have lined up some human volunteers to take part in our practice today." Mrs. Robertson motioned to the doorway. Twelve men and five women walked into class. "I'm afraid I'm one person short, not realizing I would have a new student. Now, these ladies and gentlemen will tell you what's bothering them, and you'll clear their mind of their worries. Depending on how strong your spell-casting ability is, they can lose their memories of the concern anywhere from a few minutes to several hours."

Turning to the purple chalkboard, she scribbled the spell on it. "Now, choose a human volunteer to work with, and when everyone's finished, we'll see how well you did."

Chairs scraped along the linoleum floor. But instead of Kate targeting a human, she headed straight for Dominic.

I tried to intercept her, but the teacher said, "It's all right, Kate. If anyone is unsuccessful with the spell, we'll give Dominic a try."

"As a new student, wouldn't it be better if he was given a chance to try first? I'll give up *my* volunteer to let him go first."

"Well, certainly. That's thoughtful of you, dear."

Thoughtful, my foot. Kate knew Dominic was a vampire. Not a warlock. She was certain he would fail. My blood absolutely sizzled with annoyance.

Dominic bowed his head slightly to Kate. A slim smile crept across his face. He turned to one of the men while I took my place in front of one of the women. I tried to concentrate on asking my volunteer what she was worrying about so I could rid her of the concern, while trying to ignore Dominic's work beside me. I needed first to clear *my* worry, but I doubted the spell would work on me, as anxious as I felt.

The tall, gangly woman, wearing a long black dress, towered over me by a good six inches. Her black hair was pulled severely back in a bun, and she appeared pale, except for the bright red lipstick coating her thin lips. She definitely looked like an older Goth. She studied me for a moment, then said only for my ears, "My concern, witch, is that you will not suffer enough at my master's command."

Instantly, my skin chilled as if I'd been immersed in an icy pool of water. The blood rushed in my ears, I forgot the spell, and the bones in my legs dissolved.

Everything after that seemed to happen all at once.

A throaty hiss escaped Dominic's lips, Kate gasped, and my female volunteer lunged at me with a wickedly sharp dagger.

9

Dominic

I COULDN'T HELP MYSELF, Prince of Darkness that I was. Marissa was mine to protect, as I was hers. When I heard the whispered words of one of Lynetta's human hosts threatening Marissa, I couldn't control my vampiric reaction. The hiss escaped my lips before I could stop it. Kate heard, so did the host and Marissa. Luckily, everyone else was too far away and preoccupied, the warlocks and witches working their own calming spells while their human volunteers waited patiently for the results.

As soon as I swung around to face the threat, the female blood host thrust a ten-inch blade at Marissa's heart. Both Marissa and I grabbed the host's arm with vampiric speed and jerked it upward. The host screamed, the teacher screamed, Kate screamed, and the dagger flew into the air.

With her hand to her breast, Mrs. Robertson said, "Please be careful with the volunteer, dears. It's only a simulation."

It was no more a simulation than my kissing Marissa had been the night before. My mind raged with fury, and I had to fight the urge to tear the woman's throat out while I fought to keep my already extended canines concealed. The overwhelming desire to use them while countermanding that urge was giving me a painful crick in the jaw.

Marissa, on the other hand, quickly worked her spell on the woman, clearing her thoughts of what she had in mind to do to Marissa.

Kate seemed to be intent on doing the same to the female host. Maybe they could wipe her mind of everything, forever. I gave a tight smile and helped them. With the three of us clearing the woman's mind, perhaps we would take care of one of Lynetta's playthings for the time being.

The teacher spoke to me, her tone saccharine sweet. "Did you finish with your volunteer, Mr. Dominic?"

"Yes, ma'am," I said, hoping I'd managed to do the spell properly before Marissa's assailant had garnered my attention.

I turned to the man I had worked with and silently commanded him to take Lynetta's blood host to the bus station, buy a ticket for her and send her to New York City. The host could wander around there for a good long while, trying to figure out what was up.

Lynetta would have lost one of the minions who was doing her evil bidding.

When the man took the woman's arm and led her from the room, the teacher smiled. "Well, they seemed pleased. I'm sorry we didn't have anyone for you to work on, Miss Kate."

Kate exchanged glances with Marissa and me. "I think I can do the spell all right."

I would love to read Kate's mind. She seemed to ponder what had happened, and I believe she had come to the conclusion I was not totally bad after all.

When the rest of the students finished their spells and the bell rang for our next class, she dogged Marissa's and my steps out the door.

"Okay, tell me the truth, you two. I want to know everything." Kate grabbed Marissa's arm and mine and pulled us out of the students' path.

"The truth is we're going steady," Marissa said, her eyes narrowed.

My stomach tightened while we waited for Kate's response, which I was sure would be explosive.

"When did this happen? While he was biting you into submission?" Her teeth clenched, Kate pointed at the fading bite marks on Marissa's neck.

Again, I felt guilty about having left any sign of what I'd done on Marissa's tender skin.

Crossing her arms, Marissa chuckled. "He can't control me, if that's what you're worried about."

Kate groaned out loud. "Are you hearing yourself?"

I was pretty sure I'd convinced Marissa to be mine, but now with Kate's interrogation of her and the anger she exhibited, my surety was slipping.

"Yes, Kate. He needs my help. And I'm going to give it to him." Marissa seemed bound and determined to stick by my side, thank heavens.

"He needs a mistress for all eternity, and you're the one, right? Until he sees a cuter girl, and then she's the one? How many centuries has this gone on? How many has he kissed into submission and heaven knows what else?"

Marissa laughed.

Her girlfriend had accused me of all kinds of hideous things, and my steady laughed?

"Well, truthfully, Kate, I think the only terrible thing he has done was give the last girl a kiss—"

"The one before that," I reminded her. "You were the last one I kissed, and it was not a terrible thing."

Marissa grinned at me. "Yes, my mistake. The girl he kissed before me was a vampire—Lynetta. She looks about the same age as us, but I think she's much older."

"Three hundred years," I supplied, wondering how I could have gotten tangled up with a woman that old.

Kate's mouth dropped open as she stared at me, her eyes emerald daggers, her cheeks crimson. "You can't ask Marissa to help you. You'll get her killed. What was this business with the human moments ago?" She waved wildly at the classroom behind us.

"That was one of Lynetta's human blood hosts. She feeds off them but doesn't share her blood with them. They remain tied to her, but not turned. She uses them to do her bidding while she sleeps," I explained.

Kate folded her arms and scowled at me. "Great. So now these hosts will come after Marissa and try to kill her? Break up with Marissa! Let the vamp know you have no interest in her, and she'll leave Marissa alone. If you care about Marissa as much as you seem to…"

"He can't, Kate." Marissa touched her shoulder. "He needs my help. If I don't kill the vamp, she'll turn him for good."

Kate stared at Marissa. "Kill her? You have to kill her?"

Marissa nodded.

Turning to face me again, Kate said, "You're only partially a…a—"

"Prince of Darkness," I offered with a slight bow.

"That's why you can be out in the sunlight."

"On a cloudy day," Marissa corrected.

Kate sternly wrinkled her brow. "You didn't stay with Marissa all last night, did you?"

I wasn't prepared for that question. And I was sure Marissa

would want to deny the truth of the matter. But when she spoke, I was shocked to hear her say what she did.

"Kate, I have never lied to you before and I don't intend to now. But you must believe me when I say that Dominic and I are bound to each other. Whether it's fate or whatever, it doesn't matter. The fact is Lynetta tried to take more of his blood last night, and I had to beat her off with a garden stake." Kate flinched, but Marissa continued. "Between that, using a release spell, and Dominic's struggles, we managed to break free from her and enter the safety of my house. He couldn't have left last night, not with her hungering outside for his blood."

"Instead, he took some of yours?" Again, Kate looked at the telltale bites on Marissa's throat.

I could tell by the bitterness in Kate's voice that she wasn't pleased with me, or how I had endangered her friend's life. But for now, I kept quiet, letting Marissa explain, as Kate had been her friend for years, not mine. I hoped beyond hope Kate would understand. As much as I desired to protect Marissa from everyone and everything, I had to give her some control over her life that I'm sure she felt she'd lost when I stepped into it.

"He had to, or grow weaker. Tonight, when she returns for him—"

Kate threw her hands up in the air in exasperation and groaned again. "I can't believe this." She fisted her hands on her hips. "You can't plan to keep him at your house again tonight."

"I can't allow her to be alone," I interjected.

"Marissa can come to *my* house."

"No," Marissa said firmly. "I can't endanger you and your family, too."

Kate paced back and forth on the walk, pausing when the warning bell rang for the beginning of the next class. She turned to Marissa. "I'm sleeping over with you."

Kate surprised the heck out of me. Marissa had a true and loyal friend in her and my admiration for Kate rose.

Marissa's eyes widened. "No," she whispered. "You can't, Kate. Lynetta will come after you, too."

Kate smiled a sort of evil grin. "I already helped you to wipe the mind of one of her hosts. I can do it again. Besides, you've helped me get out of some tough binds with guys..." She glanced at me as if I were in that category, then faced Marissa again. "So I owe you."

"But Lynetta's evil to the core. I—"

"Either you let me in on this...or I'll let it slip to my parents that you have a guy staying at your house. They'll tell your aunt. She'll tell your parents. You know how that'll turn out." Kate slipped her arm through Marissa's and walked her toward the potions class. "Deal?" She glanced back at me.

"The more the merrier," I said, figuring we hadn't any choice. And maybe, just maybe, one more witch could help us.

Wouldn't Lynetta be surprised?

Marissa shook her head. *"I don't want her involved! It's not safe for her. Well, for any of us, but we can't help what we have to do. She still has a choice."*

"Agreed."

"You do realize," I said, attempting to dissuade Kate for Marissa's peace of mind, "we'll have to destroy Lynetta?"

Kate's lips turned up. "Yeah, well when a girl tries to steal another's soul mate, I would say it's a fair proposition."

Marissa stared wordlessly. Then she frowned. "You don't know what you're getting yourself into."

"Well, I imagine when drop-dead gorgeous kissed you last night, you didn't either." Kate looked back at me and winked.

Women. If I live a thousand years, I will never be able to figure them out. First, she hated my guts, and now, I was drop-dead gorgeous?

When we walked into potions class, a grizzled old male teacher motioned to tables where beakers and jars of ingredients sat. "You're late," he said abruptly, bushy white brows knitted in a scowl. Gnarled fingers combed through the white beard extending to his knees. He didn't even seem to notice I was new to class.

"You're late," he repeated, and we hurried to take the only three unoccupied seats at the front of the class.

Marissa turned to me. *"He spits when he speaks. Loose dentures. Everyone avoids sitting up front."*

I wrinkled my nose. She stifled a laugh.

The teacher said, "Everyone was to have ingredients for the sleeping potion."

"Invisibility potion, Mr. Thornton," Kate reminded him.

He stared at her for a moment, cleared his throat, then nodded. "Yes, right, the invisibility potion. You learned the procedure last week, but now that you have your ingredients, you can put it to practice. The test is open book."

Marissa looked at me, concern etched in the wrinkle of her brow. *"I don't have enough ingredients for both of us."*

"I don't need the potion to turn invisible."

"Right. We can just make something up."

Marissa opened her book and began to slip her ingredients into the bottle. Kate glanced at me, then realizing I didn't have anything to put in mine, shoved some roots, a grassy-looking substance, a vial of yellow liquid and three mushrooms to me.

Surprised, but immeasurably pleased, I bowed my head to her, wordlessly thanking her. After adding the proper amounts to the beaker, I handed the rest back to her with my profound gratitude.

"Partners in crime," she whispered and gave me a wry smile.

I realized then, somehow, I'd won Marissa's best friend over, too, which could only help our situation at this point.

After adding boiling water to the mixture, stirring and shaking the ingredients until they dissolved into a fine liquid, we were to test the potion on ourselves. I raised the cooled beaker to my lips but couldn't force myself to drink the obnoxious-smelling potion, bittersweet and slightly acidic. I pretended to drink it, then set the beaker on the table. With a motion of my hand, I vanished. Then so did Marissa.

"Can you sense me here beside you, Marissa?"

"You're invisible."

I felt the warmth of her body, smelled the perfume scenting her, and listened to the subtle increase in the beat of her heart. I would have reached out and pulled her to me, but I wanted her to learn how to find me on her own when she was invisible.

"Yes, I'm invisible, but can you feel my presence? Shut your eyes and use your sixth sense to locate me."

She drew closer, her breath touching my cheek, her heart beating faster. I moved my lips to hers and smiled when her mouth turned up.

"I sense you are very close, Dominic."

"Hmmm, yes, you have great sensory perception."

I kissed her like I had the night before, building up the passion, gently at first. She hummed her pleasure when I kissed her eyelids, her cheeks, then worked down to her lips.

Suddenly, the sound of clapping filled the room.

10

M ARISSA

WITH OUR LIPS LOCKED TOGETHER, my eyes popped open. Dominic and I were fully visible. My cheeks burned—well, so did my whole body, all the way down to my sneaker-covered toes.

Mr. Thornton stared at us for a moment, then his gray cheeks stained cherry and he coughed. "Now you can see where the invisibility potion can come in handy. Only next time, you might want to make it a might more powerful to make the experience last longer."

I glanced at Kate, expecting to see disapproval. But instead, she smiled at me. Did she now understand? For once in my life, a guy cared about me, and only about me. It warmed me through and through.

"Yeah," she said, "I would say he's a keeper, girl."

"That's what I thought." I grinned at her, totally thrilled she seemed to like him too, and wanted the best for me.

Mr. Thornton explained the ingredients we would require for our next potion and how to combine them to produce the perfect sleeping aid.

When the bell rang, it was time for history. Dominic and I nearly slept through class while Miss Winston droned on about the Salem witch trials, absent-mindedly twisting a gray curl around her finger the whole time. But when it came to the last class for the day, gym, Dominic tried to follow Kate and me into the witches' locker room. I pointed at the room across the hall. "Warlocks' locker room."

He rubbed his chin and considered the door to the guys' locker room. "You know, I'm not really a jock or anything."

I squeezed his hand, hoping to reassure him it didn't matter to me. "You don't have to be but try not to do anything you shouldn't. After this, school's done."

"Lunchtime?" His dark brows perked up.

"Yep." I was glad to see his spirits lifted.

"Good, I'm already famished."

"Are you buying?"

Dominic smiled. "I thought you were cooking."

"We'll order a pizza," Kate said, then tugged me toward the locker room. Dominic looked so forlorn, I balked. "He'll live."

But then I saw Debbie Damint headed for the girls' locker room, her attention riveted toward Dominic, her girlfriends Linnie and Carissa in tow—a disaster just waiting to happen.

I must have looked livid because Kate glanced from me to the girls and said, "What's up, Marissa?"

"Debbie turned Dominic into a toad a while back."

Kate's brows rose and she snapped her gaping mouth shut.

"I can't make them forget they've seen him before. Though I

sure wish I could," I said, not sure of any options I might have, but I started walking toward Dominic.

He caught sight of the three witches who were now bearing down on him, his attention focused on them so much he didn't know I was coming up behind him. Her lipstick as red as her hair, Carissa glanced in my direction and gave me a "what-do-you-want?" kind of look.

I ignored her and seized Dominic's arm. Pulling him around, I smiled to see his eyes rounded in surprise. "I didn't give you a parting kiss."

I tried to ignore the audience of witches and concentrate on the kiss. Dominic jumped right in and helped me with a sexy, lingering, sizzling hot kiss and by the time we broke free, I was sure my cheeks were rose-red. Wow, what a kisser.

For a minute, I felt like I might swoon, and Dominic held my arm to keep me upright, then pressed his lips against my cheek and whispered, "You sure know how to send a guy to the moon, Marissa. See you in a little bit."

Dominic winked at Kate, whose cheeks colored crimson and mouth hung slightly agape. I chanced a look at Debbie Damint and her friends. Carissa's red brows were arched to her bangs, and her arms were crossed over her chest. Linnie tucked her dark hair behind her ear, but her eyes were still wide with surprise. Debbie Damint looked from me to Dominic, and I wondered if she was thinking she'd made one horrible mistake turning such a hunk into a toad.

As soon as I grabbed Kate's arm and hurried her to the girls' locker room while Dominic disappeared into the boys' locker room, Debbie caught up with me. "Hey, what's going on with this guy?"

I attempted to look like I didn't know what she was talking about and lifted one shoulder in response.

She glanced back at her girlfriends, but both seemed tongue-tied.

"He's not a warlock," Debbie insisted.

"Oh?" I said, with a definite lift to my brows and voice.

"Yeah, he...I...we would have known."

"Cloaking," I lied. "He has a rare ability to cloak his gifts." I gave her the most winsome smile, intimating I had captured the attention of a warlock extraordinaire. Which I had, so there on them.

Kate instantly joined in on the game. "Yeah," she said dreamily, her hands pressed to her heart. "I would give anything to have a guy like that interested in me."

I loved that she was really good at going along when she got the gist of a game in play.

Debbie glanced at her friends.

Linnie shrugged. "I don't know. I've never heard of such a thing."

Carissa sneered. "I don't believe it."

"Well, whatever. He's new to school, and when we met at the Hamburger Spot..." I paused for effect, sighed deeply and continued, "...we just gravitated toward each other. Our fate was written in the stars. Good thing he hadn't met any other witches first. Boy, was I ever lucky."

"He didn't even try to stop you," Linnie said to Debbie.

"Stop what?" Kate asked, her eyes narrowing, pretending she didn't know that Debbie and her friends had done something bad to Dominic.

"That's what makes him the kind of guy he is," I said, entering the locker room. "You know, the type who would put up with people's nonsense and not turn them into worms for being so mean-hearted."

"What happened?" Kate asked, her voice rising in exasperation, playing her part perfectly, and for once I thought she wasn't a half bad actress after all.

"Nothing," Debbie said quickly. Her face was pale, and she hurried off to her locker.

Linnie cast a glance at me, then quickly closed the gap between her and Debbie. Carissa just stared at me, as if she was trying to intimidate me into telling the truth.

"Want something?" I asked, totally superior-like.

"He's human."

"Really? Well, I wonder how he got into our school, then. Better watch out because if you try anything with him, you might be the one wearing the bumpy, slimy skin instead."

Carissa's mouth opened as though she intended to say something, but then she whipped around and stalked off instead.

"What was that all about?" Kate whispered.

"Another of Dominic's mistakes," I said, my voice hushed. And I wondered then how many others he'd made where girls were concerned.

"Okay, so Debbie turned him into a toad, why?"

"He asked her out to the movies."

Kate chuckled. "He sure gets himself into fixes."

"I don't think they'll bother him again."

"Ohmigod, no. I thought all three of them were going to die when he kissed you so long and hard. Does he have a brother by chance?"

I gave Kate a smug smile. "I didn't expect him to give that much of a show in front of them, but it seemed to work." Then I frowned at Kate when we reached our lockers, determined to find out her role in the Joshua situation. "What in the world did you say to Joshua to get him to pay attention to me?"

"What? Nothing." Kate sounded sincere but grouchy Iwould even suggest such a thing.

"You didn't bribe him to offer to take me to the dance?"

Kate shook her head, stripped out of her jeans, and pulled on navy gym shorts. "I thought he was hung up on Debbie Damint."

"Well, something got into him because all of a sudden he asked to carry my bag and offered to take me to the dance. He got really perturbed that Dominic said he was my steady."

"Jeez, how did Dominic handle it?"

I pulled the gray gym shirt over my head. "Not well. Joshua threatened to take him on during gym class."

Kate frowned. "I hope Dominic has lots of self control. I mean, when he hissed in class earlier, I nearly had a heart attack. As soon as I saw his sharp canines appear and of course when he defended you against that woman..." Kate shuddered. "I could see he really cares for you—deeply, I mean. Well, heck, the way he kissed you..." She gave a heavy sigh. "Gosh, are you lucky."

I considered Kate's words about Dominic's control, then shook my head. He wouldn't let Joshua egg him on. "I'll only be lucky if we can destroy the vamp."

Kate nodded and pulled her hair back in a scrunchy. "Otherwise, he'll become one of them for real, right?"

"Worse." I really didn't want to discuss what would happen if we didn't win the game, but I couldn't hide the truth from my best friend. Especially when she was willing to risk her own life to help us.

"What can be worse than that?" Kate asked, her eyes dark with concern.

I tied up my hair and took a deep breath. "He's my soul mate. If he's turned, he'll still come after me."

"Oh, great. And turn you?" Kate chewed on her bottom lip.

"Yeah." No way could I tell her he'd already managed to do that to me to an extent. But I suspected once we destroyed Lynetta, the curse would be lifted for both Dominic and me.

Certainly, there wasn't any reason to mention what had happened to me, not at this point.

"But, Marissa, don't you think we ought to ask some experienced, more powerful witches and warlocks for help?"

"Would any believe us? You believed it could be true because you already suspected he was a Prince of Darkness. Even I had a hard time with it, until…" I stared at the floor, the image of Lynetta's wicked teeth still poised to strike Dominic's throat filling my mind.

"Marissa?"

I looked up at Kate through misty eyes. The sight of the soul-less eyes of the vamp was burned into my memory. "When Lynetta extended her canines, intent on piercing Dominic's throat—"

Kate nodded. "You couldn't deal with her attempting to hurt him because you already knew he was yours."

"Yeah. But how could I?" I really wasn't into the fate thing. Even now, I couldn't see it as providence, just that we were drawn to each other, like any guy and girl might be. He needed my help, and I was willing to come to his aid. That was all.

"You sensed him in the dark, when I couldn't."

I swallowed hard, remembering how strange it felt to know he was hidden in the dark, watching us, and Kate hadn't sensed him at all. "That's what *he* said."

"So, does he have a brother?"

Not sure if she was joking or not, I frowned at Kate. She often had a wry sense of humor, but I really wasn't sure this time.

She smiled. "Just kidding. Let's play ball."

Mrs. Sticklemire tied her red hair back with a ribbon, straightened her gray T-shirt, stiffened her spine and motioned for us to all line up against the bleachers. Which meant she would lecture us, again.

"Yesterday we had a rather embarrassing incident when one of the boys cast a magic spell to win a game and accidentally broke another boy's leg. You girls are much better behaved."

The girls grinned.

"But after yesterday's fiasco, the principal told us we had to explain the rules again. Physical training is just that. Exercising your bodies and giving your brains a rest. Therefore, just like regular human students do, our P.T. program is strictly for exercise. All witches and warlocks are forbidden to cast any spell during P.T." Mrs. Sticklemore tossed the rubber ball to Debbie Damint. "Let's begin."

Debbie Damint threw the colorful ball, trying to tag another player while I attempted to read Dominic's thoughts. I couldn't help but worry about him with Joshua. I could just imagine Joshua egging him on until Dominic's teeth extended.

"Try one more time, warlock." I read Dominic's thoughts and figured his feelings had to be aimed at Joshua.

Before I could worry anymore about that, the ball hit me squarely in the chest, knocking me down. I let out a strangled "oof" in surprise.

"Oh, sorry, Marissa!" Debbie called out, her tone totally apologetic.

I sighed. Beautiful, brainy, athletic, and good-natured, the girl had no faults. Except that Dominic had been attracted to her and she'd turned him into a toad—which was totally unacceptable in witch/warlock circles. She really was the perfect person to hate.

Kate ran to help me up. "Are you all right?"

"Take me to the healer's station," I whispered, holding my chest, pretending it hurt worse than it did, knowing the tips of my ears had to be brilliant red from fibbing. But I was sure as hard as I'd fallen, the teacher would think I might have been more seriously injured.

"Take her," Mrs. Sticklemire said, her red brows pinched, motioning for Kate to hurry.

I was certain my teacher was perturbed anyone would get injured in her class after the mess with the boys yesterday. But at least it was just because of my not paying attention and not because anyone had broken the rules.

Kate helped me to the locker room, then I bolted for the boys' gym room. "Marissa, what's going on?"

"Dominic's had his fill of Joshua!" I couldn't tell her I worried he would threaten Joshua with his fangs, and already I was close to panicking.

"Oh, great!" Kate exclaimed, the exasperation evident in her voice.

The shortest way to the boys' gym was through their locker room. And since all the boys would still be in the gym, I dashed through there, diving between the labyrinth of red and blue metal lockers with Kate breathing down my neck. The odor of smelly socks and sneakers and chlorinated shower water permeated the air.

Suddenly male voices spoke, some laughing, some in heated argument, as their sneaker-clad feet clomped in our direction.

"Back," I whispered to Kate. Her face turned snow white, and she whirled around and ran back to the entrance.

I wished I could stop whatever Joshua would pull with Dominic, and wished I had an invisibility potion so I could help defend him with my witch's powers without Joshua or Dominic knowing. I wished so hard my arms, my legs and my whole body vanished in a flash before my very eyes. I was thrilled and terrified!

Turning invisible just by wishing it was just too cool, but what if I wished for it at the wrong time? Not really wanting it, but just thinking how nice it would be and *poof,* I vanished?

This could be *so* bad.

I felt as solid as before, just like when using the invisibility potion, except no sweet acidic taste accompanied the change. Then another notion nagged at me. How long would it last?

All I would need was for someone to catch me in the locker room and report me to the staff.

Then Dominic appeared, Joshua following him, crowding him, violating his space. I couldn't hear his words, but Dominic's face grew dark with anger.

Then he seemed to sense I was nearby. He shook his head at me. *"Go, Marissa. I'll deal with this in my own way."*

His thoughts were harsh, and he definitely didn't want me to interfere. What was going on with Joshua?

"Marissa, go." Dominic frowned in my direction. *"If you see a naked guy in here, you'll lose your concentration and turn visible. Then what will you do?"*

I didn't want to leave him alone. Not if I could help him against Joshua.

Ignoring me when I wouldn't obey, Dominic turned to face him. "Why are you interested in dating Marissa all of a sudden? Why wait ten years before you take any notice of her?"

Joshua yanked off his sweaty T-shirt and opened his mouth to speak, but then a boy walked into the room wearing only a towel around his waist, the rest of him dripping wet, and I inadvertently gasped.

Dominic swung around, his face hard, his eyes as dark as a brewing thunderstorm.

I ran for the locker room's entrance, my tennis shoes clomping on the floor.

Laughter filled the air. "Hey, who's the witch sneaking a peek at us naked boys?" one of the guys hollered.

If I hadn't been so scared about getting caught, I would have laughed.

"My very own Marissa," Dominic thought to himself. *"I've created a wild woman."*

"In your dreams, Prince of Darkness."

"Yeah, you are, Marissa, my love. You are."

As soon as I bolted out of the room, Kate grabbed my arm. "Tell me you didn't get caught."

"I didn't." My mouth was cotton dry, and I headed to the water fountain.

"Tell me the truth now." Kate trailed behind me. "Your face is as red as a chili pepper, and I imagine just as hot."

"I swear, I didn't get caught." I drank my fill from the fountain, but that didn't satisfy the dryness of my throat.

Kate grabbed my arm, hauling me toward the girls' locker room. "Jeez, Marissa, let's get changed and go home for the day. I can't take any more excitement than this."

"Wait until tonight," I warned her.

"Yeah, I forgot."

I turned when I heard someone's footsteps behind us.

Joshua cast a knowing smile at me from the boys' locker room entrance. What had gotten into him?

"Having regrets?" Kate asked me, pulling me into the girls' room.

I shook my head. "No." I didn't either. Not yet.

After we changed back into our street clothes and left the girls' gym, Dominic joined us. He shook his head at me, a glint of a sparkle in his dark eyes.

"What?"

"You didn't need to rescue me." He took Kate's book bag and mine, then slung them over his shoulders.

"You were angry with Joshua," I countered, still unable to squash the worry about the bad blood between them. It seemed utterly ridiculous, too, because Joshua had never shown any interest in me before. So why now?

"I controlled my temper."

"Well, I worried about you."

He took my hand and squeezed lightly. "I know." His words were warm, and though he seemed perturbed that I had tried to rescue him, I could tell my actions touched him.

We passed the wooded park where joggers ran on an asphalt path and kids too young for school played in an airy fortress, complete with slides, rope ladders, and bright yellow, blue and red tunnels.

Kate glanced behind her. "Uhm, while you guys were busy making up, I think we picked up a couple of stalkers."

Dominic and I looked over our shoulders. Two men dressed all in black, like a couple of overgrown Goths, were closing the gap between us, though they still had about a football-sized field to go.

"Use your protection spells." Dominic hurried us along.

"Will it work against them?" I quickly raised my fingers to create the spell, while Kate mimicked my actions.

"They might be human hosts, or just a couple of guys out for a stroll." Despite speaking calmly, his words had a tinge of worry to them.

I looked up at Dominic, my eyes searching his for the truth. "What if they're like you, Dominic? What if they're partly turned and can move around in the daylight?"

"Use your protection spells," he reiterated. His avoidance of my question troubled me.

Did he know these men? I couldn't read his thoughts as though a brick wall suddenly rose between us. Not knowing what he felt or what he thought sent panic hurtling through me.

He squeezed my hand, then warned, "Run, ladies, run!"

My heart lodged in my throat, but I ran for my house like he commanded.

Kate sprinted like a deer while I tried to catch up, and

Dominic protected us from the rear, or so I thought. Kate suddenly screamed when one of the men appeared in front of her.

"Vampires!" I cried out, realizing at once that was what they truly were.

Kate stepped backward, but to my surprise, the man didn't advance.

I turned to look for Dominic, but he and the other man had vanished. "We're on our own, Kate," I whispered.

"Just like a man. The going gets rough—"

"And the tough hightail it out of here so the women can handle the trouble."

I couldn't figure out why the vampire wasn't attacking, though. Maybe our protection spell? "Try the 'you-know-what' we did in Mrs. Robertson's class today."

"Ah, the—"

"Yes."

We both attempted casting the spell on him, trying to wipe his mind of what he intended to do to us. He jerked his head back as if he were trying to fight our efforts.

I remembered how Dominic had commanded the volunteer he worked with in class to send the host to New York City. I didn't have any money to bus this guy anywhere. Instead, I commanded him to walk to Disney World and ride the roller coaster at Space Mountain two hundred times. I didn't know if my suggestion would wear off shortly or what, but the man began walking in an easterly direction.

"Come on!" I grabbed Kate's arm and we sprinted for my house.

After unlocking the door, we rushed inside, then bolted it shut.

"Dominic." I couldn't curb the crushing thought he was in

terrible danger while the adrenaline still pulsed through my body at an all-time high.

Kate squeezed my hand with reassurance. "He'll be all right, Marissa. I just know it."

But I didn't. I couldn't sense anything from him. Not one feeling at all. He'd disappeared into a black void of space and my heart felt like it was ripped out and sucked into the abyss with him.

11

D OMINIC

IN A DEEPLY WOODED area next to a swollen creek, about a mile from Marissa's housing development, I faced the newly-turned vampire—though in truth I was still only a fledgling myself. Dressed in jeans and a matching jacket, the tall blond stared at me with bleak gray eyes. Thankfully, he kept his teeth sheathed. I assumed it was only because Lynetta had ordered no harm was to come to me. But in the secluded woods, I was prepared to do battle if need be.

With all my heart, I hoped Marissa and Kate were all right. I was relieved Marissa had told her friend the truth about us. Together, two witches more than likely could deal with the lone vampire. I wasn't sure Marissa could have handled him by herself, with as little confidence as she had in her witch's spells.

The vampire seemed hesitant to tackle me, and I wasn't willing to make the first move, not yet.

Suddenly, the thought occurred to me that the man who faced me didn't realize I had the advantage. Thinking I was a human-turned-vampire like him, he had no idea I had Marissa's gift and was now a warlock-turned-vampire.

The man must have been in his thirties, as evidenced by the stockier build of his body and the light crow's feet at the edges of his eyes when he squinted. His beady eyes seemed to grow even smaller as he glared at me.

Had Lynetta turned to older men to do her dirty work? It appeared so. But she'd sworn I was to be her only mate forever. For a second, it bugged me. Then I had to laugh at my idiocy when I pondered the matter further. I didn't care for her, so what difference did it make if she sought out other guys?

"What do you want?" I asked, surveying the empty woods to ensure there were no others readying to attack me. Figuring it would be advantageous to lure one of the men away from the girls, I'd urged him to follow me to this private place and hoped my plan was a good one. The breeze whooshed through the leaves of the oaks, birds chattered in the treetops, and the fragrance of pine scented the air. Nothing hinted at the evil that lurked in the bloodsucker's heart as he stood several feet away from me.

"If you come with me without a fight, Lynetta will leave your girlfriend alone."

"What guarantee do I have?" I considered the notion briefly, not because I believed him, but because now that I was a warlock, I wondered if I had a chance to kill Lynetta on my own. Since I couldn't control a witch's or warlock's thoughts, could she, being the ancient vampire she was, still control me? The idea I might be able to save myself without involving Marissa in the deadly business held a definite allure.

"Will you come with me?" the man asked, his words hopeful, but edged with a threat.

"I would love to, but I already have a lunch date." With the loveliest girl I had ever met. Besides, I figured if I went with him, I would find a house filled with vampires and wouldn't stand a chance. They would keep me there for Lynetta, and she would take her revenge out on me, and on Marissa and Kate. I didn't trust her not to. My stomach knotted, along with my fists.

He paused for a second, then bared his teeth. I assumed my reply didn't meet with his approval. Instantly, I tried the mind-clearing spell. His canines slipped back into their sheaths, the elongated teeth now their normal human size. He seemed confused, and I nearly laughed, only the business at hand was too dangerous to consider lightly. Marissa's passing her gift of magic skills to me was further proof she was my savior.

"Do you have a credit card?" I asked, extremely cocky now that I thought I had everything under control.

He pulled out his wallet, then looked through it. Seizing a credit card, he held it up, a silly grin plastered on his face.

"Very good." I refrained from speaking to him like he was an obedient dog to be praised with a pat on his bony head, but the thought did cross my mind. "I command you to go to the Waco airport and buy a ticket to...Australia." I figured that would give him a nice long flight. "You will get on the flight to Dallas, then transfer planes until you make your way to Sydney. Once there, you will find an apartment and stay."

The wearing off of the mind-clearing spell might occur faster, but controlling a human, even if partially-turned, was easy and lasted indefinitely, unless someone else with vampiric abilities controlled him. But now that I was a warlock...

I smiled—I had even more abilities than before. Marissa couldn't have aided me any better if she'd tried. *Marissa!* My heart plummeted, thinking of the difficulties she and Kate might be facing.

"Go!" I ordered, and with a wave of his hand, he disappeared.

With a wave of mine, I vanished from the woods and reappeared in Marissa's living room.

First, high-pitched, ear-shattering screams from two frightened witches in reaction to my sudden appearance filled the room. Then hugs and kisses from both were bountifully bestowed on me.

I could *really* get used to this.

Then Marissa slugged me in the shoulder with her fist. "Where did you disappear to? You had us worried sick."

Unable to take her punch seriously, I gave her a small smile. But the fact she had worried about me made my heart soar. "I wanted to separate the vampires and thought it safer if the two of you only had one to tackle."

"Hmpf." Marissa folded her arms.

I kissed her lips, and she immediately wrapped her arms around me and gave me another wonderful squeeze. Her perky breasts brushed against my chest, stirring my hormones to high heaven.

"What happened?" Kate asked, her voice still concerned.

To my annoyance, her words temporarily broke the spell Marissa had over me. "The vampire I took care of is taking a trip to Australia. And yours?"

"A trip to Disney World," Marissa explained, her hand stroking my arm.

My heart already beat out of control, and my body reacting to her touch would soon embarrass me. "That's not very far. A few hours to fly at the most."

She smiled. "He's walking."

I was momentarily speechless. She got the vampire to walk there? *Bravo!*

She read my thoughts and her lips curved up. "And when he arrives, he's going to ride Space Mountain two hundred times."

I laughed out loud. "You sure know how to punish a guy."

"Yeah, so just remember that and don't get on my bad side."
She teasingly poked me in the ribs with one finger.

Kate stared at Marissa as if she'd sprouted bat's wings.

Marissa frowned at her. "What's wrong, Kate?"

"I thought you just wiped his mind of his thoughts, like I did.
We haven't learned any spell that'll control a person's mind and
make them do what you did. In fact, I don't believe we can do
any such thing."

Kate didn't know the whole story and was bound to be angry
when she heard it. Again, I felt compelled to let Marissa do the
explaining on her own.

Marissa cleared her throat and took Kate's hand. "We hadn't
meant for it to go this far...well, not yet, anyway. But when we
kissed, Dominic had bitten his tongue and—"

Kate pulled her hand free and collapsed on the sofa, her face
pale. "You're one of *them* now?"

"Some of his abilities transferred to me. I can read his
thoughts, and he can read mine."

Kate glanced back at me as if seeking confirmation. I
nodded.

"I...I, well..." Marissa straightened her spine. "...I can turn
invisible without a potion. But I didn't know about it until it just
happened." She gave me a scathing look.

How would I know she would have that ability, too?

Kate rubbed her temple. "Is that how you stayed so long in
the boys' locker room without getting caught?"

Marissa glanced at me—this time her face definitely had a
guilty look. "Yes."

"Did you see anyone? I mean, naked?" Kate looked totally
intrigued, even hopeful.

Still trying to curb my annoyance that Marissa didn't believe
I could control my primal urges to knock Joshua's block off, I
said, "If she had, she would have probably lost her concentra-

tion and become visible again. As it was, Joshua and a couple of other guys heard her run out of the room. I'm sure they figured she was a witch who'd used the invisibility potion to sneak into the locker room for a peek."

Kate laughed.

Marissa's cheeks colored beautifully. I reached over and gave her a hug.

"What else can you do, Marissa?" Kate asked. Her voice had changed from one of horror to awe. I wondered if she wished she could have switched places with Marissa in the locker room.

Marissa wrinkled her forehead at me.

I chuckled inwardly, forgetting for an instant that she could read my mind. In fact, I often forgot she could read my thoughts and wasn't sure I would ever get the hang of keeping them cloaked from her.

Tilting her chin up, she shook her head at me. We exchanged knowing smiles, then she turned and answered Kate. "Well, I can control a human's mind. But not a witch's or warlock's. I can't seem to disappear and reappear in other places like Dominic can. When I saw Matthew wearing only a towel in the locker room, I had to run out of there. Vanishing like Dominic does would have been preferable, but I can't seem to do it."

Kate's green eyes were wide with excitement. "Wow. Awesome. Will you let me know if you suddenly have more abilities?"

Marissa regarded her with amusement. "Sure thing, Kate."

Kate turned her attention to me. "You don't happen to have a brother lurking about, do you?"

I knew then, she truly was part of our team. "I have an older brother, eighteen, James, really bright and is in his freshmen year at Baylor University, but he's just a plain old human. I'm sure you wouldn't be interested in him."

"Oh." Disappointment reflected in her voice.

A human wasn't an acceptable boyfriend for a witch, nor would a human wish to date a witch. The two would never in a million light years be interested in each other. Then again, unwritten rules were made to be broken.

"There are plenty of warlocks who are interested in you at school, Kate," Marissa said, her voice cheerful.

Kate eyed me. "Yeah, but none are as fun to be with as Dominic."

Liking the boost to my ego, I smiled at her.

Marissa plunked herself down on the sofa. "She's the adventurous one of the two of us, Dominic, if you hadn't guessed it already. If she found an old oil lamp, she would clean it until it sparkled to find the genie in it or kiss a frog to find her prince. She would even climb down that rabbit's hole to join Alice on her adventures in Wonderland."

"Well, Kate," I said, grabbing up the portable phone, "when things start getting really rough, you may wish you didn't sign onto *this* little adventure." I punched the numbers for my favorite pizza place, Pizzas Out of this World. "What does everyone want on their pizza?"

After deciding the kind of crust and the toppings, Kate called her parents to tell them she was having lunch with Marissa and asked if she could stay the evening. Marissa called her Aunt Betsy and told her how her day at school went, and that Kate was spending the night. I relayed to my family that I would be staying safely with a friend for a couple of more nights.

Of course, I was hoping that by Friday evening, I could give them the really good news—I was liberated from Lynetta forever. Every time I spoke to my mother, I could hear the tears in her voice, and I couldn't help but feel awful for what I was putting her through. But as much as I could, I attempted to reassure her that my new friends were going to help me, and that seemed to relieve her anxiety somewhat.

Half an hour later, the doorbell rang. Our pizza had arrived. But when Kate opened the door, both Marissa and I sensed something was wrong right away. It wasn't the uniform the pizza boy wore, though the one-size-fits-all red vest seemed two sizes too small. It wasn't the ancient vehicle he drove that carried the pizza parlor's logo lopsided on the passenger's door. Nor was it the well-worn, warming mitt colored orange instead of red that covered the large pizza box that really aroused our suspicions.

His dark brown eyes focused on Marissa with a vengeance, a glint of pure malevolence sparking in their depths. But even more than that, we both smelled the scent of fresh blood on him as if he'd just had an afternoon snack.

Kate motioned for him to come inside. Before she could utter a word, Marissa and I lunged for her.

12

M ARISSA

I WAS certain this was one adventure even my poor friend Kate wasn't ready for. My heart pounding, I slapped my hand over Kate's mouth to keep her from inviting the pizza delivery boy into my home, while Dominic slammed the door in the imposter's face.

Poor Kate. Her eyes couldn't have gotten any wider, nor could her skin have turned any whiter. She'd taken everything so well until Dominic and I reacted so violently to the pizza delivery. The thought that the vampire could have gained entry into my house and let Lynetta or any other vampire in, sent chills cascading down my spine.

"That was too close for comfort," Dominic said, eyeing both of us to ensure we weren't too shaken by the ordeal.

"Lynetta's going to keep sending them, isn't she?" I asked, hoping he would say no and settle the disquiet forming in the pit of my stomach. In my heart I knew she would come for him, her chosen. And she would destroy me, too, for trying to steal him away from her.

"Uhm, guys," Kate said, peering out the front picture window, her brow furrowed, "what do we do with the pizza delivery dude?"

To my surprise, Dominic suddenly vanished from the house and materialized next to the delivery boy. The guy nodded, climbed into his car and drove off.

This time Dominic returned to the house via the front door. "He remembered the pizza belonged to a John Smith in San Francisco, California."

Kate chuckled. "I imagine the pizza will be ice cold by the time it gets there."

Not wanting Kate to hear my question, I spoke to Dominic telepathically, the worry imprinted on my brain. *"Why did he smell of blood?"*

"He had just eaten a rat."

My head began to spin. I'm sure my face was paler than pale. "I'll be right back." I hurried for the bathroom.

Seconds later, I held my head over the toilet, grateful I made it in time and didn't have to clean up a mess in the living room. Someone rapped on the door.

"Marissa?" Dominic half-whispered, his voice threaded with concern. "Marissa, I'm sorry. I shouldn't have told you."

I wiped the tears from my cheeks and pulled the bathroom door open. "Is that what we're destined to do?"

Would I end up killing mammals, feasting on their blood, siphoning the life force from their shuddering bodies? Again, I felt the urge to return to the toilet.

"Not if we can kill Lynetta."

It all came back to that. "Just how are we to accomplish such a feat?"

Dominic sighed a ragged breath and ran his hand over my arm. "We'll find a way. We have to."

Clanging resounded in the kitchen. I raised my brows in question.

Dominic jerked his thumb in the direction of the noise. "Kate is looking for something else for us to eat."

I ran for the kitchen, the nausea in my stomach instantly subsiding as my mind focused on a new concern. "She has a chef's heart, but she burns everything she cooks." I turned to Dominic who followed close on my heels. "Inattention to the task. Easily distracted."

"I heard that!" Kate yelled out, laughter in her voice.

I sighed heavily when I saw her stirring mayonnaise and tuna fish in a mixing bowl. *Tuna fish sandwiches.* She couldn't go wrong with that.

Kate looked up from her work. "Exactly how can we kill a vampire? I've read the fictional books on it—stake to the heart, cut off their head, expose them to sunlight—anything else I've missed?"

We both looked at Dominic to hear what the authority on the subject had to say about it.

He shrugged. "I don't know."

"What do you mean you don't know?" Kate's voice rose an octave while she slathered the tuna fish-mayonnaise mixture on slices of white bread.

"Just that. I've never seen one killed. So I don't know if the fictional tales have any truth to them or not." He walked in front of the oven door sporting reflective black glass.

We could see Dominic's reflection in the glass, and I felt a bit of relief that he was still pretty human.

"See? Not all the tales are accurate."

"Ah, but what if that's because you're only partially turned?" I asked.

"Might be." He carried his plate and a glass of milk to the table. "I don't have any idea if a full-fledged vampire would have an image in a mirror or not."

I glanced at my own reflection. "What about garlic?"

"No reaction to that. My mother is a big believer in spicing food up. Unless it's a dessert dish, she adds garlic to it. I ate both her grilled chicken and lasagna last week, no problem."

"Crosses?" I asked.

He shook his head and took a drink of his milk. "Not that either. I even went to church with my brother's friend's family and experimented with holy water. No effect."

Kate cut her sandwich into quarters. "What about carrying around the dirt of your birthplace?"

"Old wives' tales," Dominic and I said at the same time.

I was really glad for that. I could just imagine trying to get a coffin-load of dirt from my birthplace in Minnesota to Texas by express mail.

Dominic lifted half of his sandwich, then paused. "I wonder if Lynetta can still control my mind now that I have some warlock abilities."

My heartbeat quickened. "Do you think she won't have control over you now?" Hope surged through me.

His eyes shimmered. "I'm going to face her on my own without involving you."

My stomach twisted. I wasn't the bravest witch on earth, but I wasn't a real scaredy cat either. Plus, what if Dominic wasn't right? What if Lynetta could still control him, even though he had gained some warlock abilities? We really had no idea what she was capable of. I couldn't let him try to tackle her on his own. Didn't he say I was his savior? That it was written in the stars? Yet the stubborn look on his face indicated he'd made up his mind.

"I *have* made up my mind, Marissa. I don't want your help in this."

I knew he was trying to protect me, so I curbed my irritation with him for dismissing me like that, but I couldn't let him fight Lynetta on his own. I could be stubborn, *very* stubborn, too. "Sorry, when you took my blood we became blood partners," I said with resolve. I fingered my uneaten sandwich, my appetite instantly crushed.

I tried to read his feelings, his thoughts, but the stone wall rose in place again. The connection I had with him instantly severed.

Yet he didn't have to tell me what he was thinking. I knew it anyway in the hard set of his jaw, the determination in his dark brown eyes. Did he plan on leaving before the cloud-veiled sun disappeared to the other side of the earth? Did he intend to face the vamp on his own?

He avoided my eyes, and I realized he was reading all my thoughts. I wished I could erect my own wall to keep him out.

He looked up at me. I smiled. He didn't want me to shut him out. I held my glass of milk to him in salute. I didn't want him shutting me out, either.

"It's for the best," he said softly.

"We don't know that, Dominic. And you can't risk it."

Up until now, Kate had reserved comment, quietly listening, mulling over the conversation. She finally said, "Let him go, Marissa. It's a guy thing. It's to prove how macho he is. Let him do what he thinks he has to do."

I couldn't believe Kate could be so...so unbelievably heartless. She had no idea how evil, how cruel Lynetta could be. No way did I want him facing the vamp on his own. I started to object. "But—"

Kate gave me one of her looks—the kind of look that said, "We'll discuss this later, when Dominic isn't around."

I wanted to argue with her, with him, to tell him to give up this foolish and dangerous plan. But I conceded. I knew in my heart he was wrong, and I could lose him forever. I also recognized he stubbornly resisted the idea that I help him now that he had his new warlock abilities and was determined to protect me at all costs.

My hands clenched in my lap, I looked down at my uneaten sandwich and tried to reconcile myself with his wishes. Then I turned to him, my own eyes moist with tears. "You still need my blood, don't you?"

His Adam's apple bobbed when he swallowed.

I sensed he thought I wouldn't offer my blood to him unless he gave up his idiotic plan. Reaching out, I took his hand. "You do what you have to do, Dominic. But I offer you my blood freely, whatever you choose to do."

His hand tightened on mine. "I can't say enough how I don't want Lynetta to hurt you."

I nodded, though I didn't have the same self-assurance he seemed to have that he would fare well with her on his own.

"I won't leave until much later tonight."

"Until we're asleep and unaware you've gone." I stated my concern as fact, with an edge to my voice. I couldn't help the anxiety building in every fiber of my being.

"I would have told you my plan, Marissa. I wouldn't have left without a goodbye kiss."

I could have screamed at him. All he wanted was a parting kiss from me?

His lips turned up sinfully sexy-like. He dropped the wall briefly to allow me to read his thoughts. *"No, dear Marissa, that is not all I want from you. But for now, while the devil lies in wait for me, I can only think about what I would like to do with you in my embrace."*

Again, the wall rose to keep me from reading his mind further. I tried to pry into his thoughts.

Dimples formed when he gave me one of his more kissable smiles. His eyes sparkled and even his dark brows rose.

A growl twisted deep inside me. I wanted to know these secret longings he had for me.

His smile broadened.

I looked away from the focus of his chocolate eyes melting with desire, my own cheeks heated to sunburn level.

"Well," Kate said grabbing up her empty plate, "want to play a board game for a while if we have no other plans like vampire extermination methods to discuss?"

No, I didn't want to play any board games! I wanted to know what Dominic had in mind to do with me.

His eyes focused on my lips. They turned up in response. He chuckled under his breath, then he helped to clear the table for the game.

Somehow, I would find a way to break down that barrier he'd put up to block me out. Also, I had to figure out a way to prevent his reading of my mind. Most of all, I had every intention of thwarting his plan to see Lynetta on his own. Somehow.

13

D OMINIC

EVEN THOUGH MARISSA wasn't happy with my plan, I had to stick to it. Keeping her safe, now that I was pretty sure I could handle Lynetta, was the only way to go.

All through the game of Magical Monopoly, which we played for several hours though I'd never played the game before—well, couldn't have, not until I had some of Marissa's magical abilities—Marissa cast sideways glances at me. A gentle nudging at my temple occurred every time she tried to probe my thoughts. Keeping my guard up against her attempts to read my mind and concentrating on the complicated game of shifting land values through the use of magic, proved to be a strain. A slight headache plagued me with the effort. If she didn't know what my plan was, she couldn't try to barge in on it, though. At least that's what I'd read she had in mind to do—not once, but several fleeting times. So I kept my defenses in place.

She was persistent, if nothing else. Again, those Caribbean blues caught my gaze. My appetite grew for her as darkness enveloped the house, but I wasn't comfortable drinking her blood in front of Kate. I'm sure the image of a vampire sucking on its chosen host looked a lot more barbaric than it felt. In actuality, the contact was totally sensual, but something that could not be explained adequately to someone who had never been bitten by a vampire. Though, when Lynetta had bitten me, her bite was a little savage—probably because she hadn't fed in so long and couldn't control her craving.

I reached over and squeezed Marissa's hand while she tapped her fingers on her lap. She looked over at me.

I opened my mind to her. *"I'm hungry."*

"Oh, dinner."

I shook my head. Dinner would be fine, of course, but I had something else in mind. Somehow, we had to seclude ourselves from Kate for a few minutes. Then I worried. *"Do you have the urge to feed also?"*

This time Marissa shook her head. I couldn't have sighed a bigger sigh of relief, and by the look on her face, she seemed to share my feelings. I leaned over and kissed her cheek.

She kissed my lips, and I wanted much more. But as I attempted to kiss her further, she rose from her chair. Already my escalating bloodlust curbed my appetite for anything but her warm, sweet blood. I'd hoped she was going to tell Kate we had to be alone for a few minutes, but instead she said, "I'll fix a pizza."

I swallowed the groan that rose from my belly. *Pizza.*

She raised her blond brows at me in a teasing fashion. *"You'll have to wait for dessert...later."*

"Tease."

"We should go to bed first."

At this last comment, my gaze raked boldly over her. The

notion of being in bed with her filled my thoughts, tangling under the sheets and comforter, kissing, touching...

She shook her head, her eyes amused.

Chagrined, I realized I'd let down my guard, and I'm sure my ears were as red-hot as they felt.

"Keep thinking those thoughts. I'll know what you're up to."

"Wild woman."

"Hmmm-hmmm."

I chuckled and Kate cast me an annoyed glance. She focused on Marissa when she shoved the pizza in the oven. "Are we having a silent conversation here without me?"

Marissa's cheeks turned scarlet, and her lips curved upward.

"Forget it. I don't *even* want to know what's being said. Or not said." Kate shrugged. "Whatever."

Yet she didn't seem perturbed that we'd left her out of the conversation. Instead, she seemed glad that she was with us tonight, in on our *adventure*, as it was.

The doorbell rang and Kate hurried to answer it. I ran my hand over Marissa's arm, then nuzzled my face against her neck. "I don't know why I'm so hungry...I mean, so much earlier than I was yesterday."

Marissa's eyes widened. "You don't think you're more turned now, do you?"

I clenched my fists, then shoved my hands in my pockets. I hadn't considered that, and my heart raced with anxiety at the thought.

"Yeah, sure, come in Joshua," Kate said, her voice enthusiastic, as if we were having a party.

Instantly, my blood boiled. Joshua? The warlock from school? Here to see Marissa? She was mine!

Already, my canines threatened to extend. With the blood-lust urging me to feed on Marissa already, I wasn't certain I could control my anger toward Joshua.

"You stay here," Marissa warned, but in a loving way, sensing there would be trouble. "I'll get rid of him."

I took a step toward the living area, ignoring Marissa's command, but she grabbed my arm. I hissed at her, and she released me at once. The look of fear in her eyes sliced through my heart.

"I...I'm sorry, Marissa. I don't know what's come over me."

She narrowed her eyes at me, a flicker of fear still marring them. "Stay here." Her words were harshly spoken, but I imagined they were the result of her being scared I would do something wretched to Joshua, maybe even to her and Kate. Or maybe she worried if she didn't use an authoritative tone, I wouldn't listen.

I truly wanted to take her in my arms and comfort her. And I wanted her blood. I clamped down on my teeth, gritted them to hold them in place.

Marissa left me in the kitchen fuming, attempting to get a grip on my hostile emotions while I paced.

"What do you want here, Joshua?" Marissa's tone was as caustic with him as it had been with me.

Good.

Joshua cleared his throat, then spoke in a persuasive, charming tone, certainly more like the way I should have talked to Marissa. My gut clenched in irritation.

"I thought we might go out for pizza tomorrow night. Then we'll go to the dance the following night," Joshua said, as if Marissa hadn't already said she wasn't interested.

"No." Marissa's tone was final. "I already told you I have plans to go with Dominic."

Now she sounded highly agitated. I was certain it irritated her that he'd never asked her out and now was forcing the issue. Was it because I was seeing her? No. He'd approached her when I was in the school administration office. I'd "heard" her talk with Kate, so knew that she hadn't bribed Joshua to ask Marissa to dance. So what was he up to?

"What kind of a fruitcake name is that anyway?" Joshua asked, now his own voice on edge.

I imagined he was not used to being turned down by a girl and being repeatedly turned down by the same one had to really irk him. Maybe that was why he persisted. He didn't like to lose. I knew the feeling well.

Silently, I paced across the tile floor, ignoring his comment, attempting to honor Marissa's wishes, avoiding the confrontation I feared would occur if I didn't. I sensed Joshua eyeing the kitchen where I, the totally useless wimp that I was, stood hiding. At that last thought, my canines extended.

"I would like for you to leave now," Marissa said in her usual diplomatic way.

I would have told the jerk to get out, now, with a few choice curses to ensure he got my meaning.

Certain he realized I was in the kitchen, I knew he baited me, hoping to bring me out in the open. Taunted me. Did he think that since I attended the average magic classes that he had the advantage? I would rip his throat apart.

"What the—" Marissa's surprised words were cut short.

I stepped into the living area to see what the matter was and got an eyeful of Joshua kissing Marissa and her hand flying toward his cheek in what would end in a painful slap.

Keeping my mouth shut to hide my extended canines, I charged across the carpeted floor, not sure what I would do when I reached them. But I was certain once I was through with Joshua, he would not *ever* pull that trick with my girlfriend again, if he even lived to tell the tale.

Joshua shoved Marissa aside as if she was garbage and not worth his time, which infuriated me more. Marissa threw her hands up in surprise, trying to keep from falling. Kate gasped. I was ready to explode.

Expecting a more physical encounter—as I'd certainly planned to get very physical with him—I was thrown off-guard when instead he voiced some kind of spell.

Both girls screamed out, "No, Joshua!"

By the time the words registered in my brain, and I realized what he had invoked, it was too late for me to react.

14

M ARISSA

As soon as Joshua cast the lightning spell, my heart stopped. The deadly bolt of white light shot down from the ceiling, striking Dominic with such force, he collapsed instantly.

Kate and I shrieked and ran to Dominic's crumpled form.

I felt for his pulse, but there was none. His face was ghastly white, and he was still as death, his hair standing up as if it was filled with thousands of atoms of static electricity. I sobbed, then turned my wrath on Joshua. "You'll be destroyed by the witches' and warlocks' council for this," I choked out.

My words sounded lame considering how devastated and infuriated I felt. I leapt to my feet, and he cast me a sinister smile, his once handsome face twisted in a mask of something vile.

The council didn't tolerate killings by warlocks or witches one bit. They allowed only the most extreme cases of self-defense, but this wasn't self-defense. This was out-and-out murder and I hoped he would fry. On the other hand, I didn't want to wait for them to get through the long procedure. I wanted to kill him myself.

The snide look on his face turned my anguish into anger. Without thinking, I attacked him. With my nonexistent nails, I attempted to rip his face while tears blurred my eyes and my heart wedged in my throat. I couldn't conjure up a spell to hurt him, I was so distraught.

Seizing my wrists, he prevented my doing any harm to him and gave me another smug grin, which stoked my anger even further. "A witch will never be as strong as a warlock," he simply said.

If I could, I would grow canines like Dominic could and rip Joshua's throat out. My whole body vibrated with anger, and I struggled to free myself from the beast so I could kill him.

Joshua responded by kissing me on the neck, shocking and sickening me. The adrenaline coursed through me, filling me with the energy to fight off the bastard. But my mind was so torn with Dominic's death, I couldn't focus my thoughts on what I had to do to Joshua.

"Now you'll go with me to the dance." Joshua shoved me aside, and I fell backwards, landing on my backside hard, knocking the breath out of me.

By the time I was back on my feet, he'd slammed the door in his hasty exodus.

He had to be mad! He'd just killed Dominic! Did he think anyone would let him get away with it?

Kate knelt at Dominic's side, holding his hand in hers. I ran to join them.

She whispered, "I didn't want to say anything while Joshua was here because he might have cast another deadly spell, but Dominic's fingers twitched a few seconds ago."

"Ohmigod! Dominic," I called to him, tears choking my throat. I squeezed his other hand but couldn't find any pulse. "Are you sure, Kate? Are you sure it wasn't just your imagination?"

"They can't die in that manner, can they? It wasn't one of the ways we discussed," Kate said, her voice calm like I wished mine could be, but her eyes were misty, too.

Staring at his lifeless form, I probed Dominic's thoughts, but there were none. His brain was as dead as his body. There was no wall to block out my probes, just nothing. I sobbed, unable to contain my grief any longer.

Kate reached over and patted my arm. "He's immortal, Marissa. Maybe it takes longer to heal after being injured so badly."

"Fatally!" I corrected her, not meaning to scream at her, but I couldn't help it. I was supposed to protect Dominic. How could I have allowed this to happen? It was all my fault Joshua decided to make a play for me. I hadn't handled anything right. Why did Dominic trust me? I was a failure at everything I did, and now...

More tears crowded down my cheeks. Now Lynetta would surely come after Kate and me, too.

Praying Kate was right, I ran my hand over his cold cheek, leaned over and listened for any sign he was breathing. Not a whisper of breath.

"I'll kill him."

"Marissa, you've got to control your emotions. Our teachers and parents drum this into us all the time—if we don't manage our feelings, we could use our witch's skills to harm someone."

"I'll kill him." I looked up at her through blurry eyes. "I'll kill Joshua for what he's done." My head throbbed with the blood rushing to it, and I was half out of my mind with a mixture of grief and anger.

"We have to let the council take care of him. But I think we need to wait before we report this to them. What if we told them he killed Dominic, then Dominic suddenly appeared just as healthy as before? We would be in some pretty hot bat guano."

I stood and left the room to concentrate better as Kate tagged along. I attempted the calming spell on myself, anything to get my anger under control.

Kate nodded, her face still tense, but she rubbed my arm, trying to console me. "That's a girl. We'll get through this somehow."

What sounded like a nearly inaudible groan came from the living room.

"Dominic!" I ran to him and fell to my knees. "Dominic!" I held his hand and kissed his cheek, my tears wetting his face.

His eyelids fluttered, but then stilled. A faint heartbeat pulsed in his wrist.

I looked up at Kate and she managed a small smile.

"Oh, Kate, maybe you're right. Let's get him up to the guest bedroom." I couldn't tell Kate what I intended to do with him. She would have to leave us alone and watch the pizza. Maybe my blood would help revive Dominic once he had come to. But I couldn't have him feed on me in front of Kate.

Before she joined us, I lifted Dominic from the floor all on my own. She stared at me in disbelief. "Maybe he's lighter from the injury," I said, trying to explain the strange phenomenon.

"Let me take him then." Kate was taller and stronger than me. Between the two of us, she would have been more capable of carrying him. But as soon as I handed Dominic's lifeless body over to her, I could see she didn't have my strength. Her knees bent as she attempted not to drop him from such a height. I immediately shoved my arms under him and lifted his weight from Kate.

"Another ability," Kate said under her breath, impressed.

"If I'm physically stronger than you," I said, my mind racing with the notion, "wouldn't I be stronger than or as strong as a warlock now?" The implication scared the hell out of me.

"I don't know. What are you thinking?"

Carrying Dominic, I started up the stairs. "Why couldn't I break free from Joshua? He reminded me witches were physically weaker than warlocks, but if I have this vampiric ability, why wouldn't I have been stronger against him?"

"Maybe your additional strength is still not strong enough to fight a warlock," Kate reasoned, but I could see she wasn't sure that was the explanation either.

"Maybe." I didn't believe it, but the other possibility I didn't *even* want to consider. What if... I shook my head. No way had Joshua been turned, too. Wouldn't he have exposed his canines?

When we reached the guest bedroom, Kate flipped on the light for me, though I didn't have the heart to tell her I didn't need it. *She* still did. Then I realized I'd forgotten to tell her about *that* new ability I had, too.

"Do you crave his blood?" Kate suddenly asked.

"No, thank God." I laid Dominic on the bed, then covered him with a pieced quilt my mother had lovingly embroidered. Never in a million years would my mother have thought a nearly dead vampire would rest beneath it a year later.

Kate sighed deeply.

I sensed her relief, but until Dominic was speaking to me, I couldn't think about anything else. "Listen, could you watch the pizza? I'm sure when it's done, Dominic might need some nourishment. But only if it isn't blackened."

Kate attempted a smile. "All right. But I don't *always* burn my cooking."

I smiled at her. "Not always." But *nearly* always.

When she left the room, I closed the door behind her and locked it.

I returned to the bed and sat on the mattress beside

Dominic. Did he still want to kiss me like he had before Joshua struck him with the lightning bolt?

"*Yes,*" he responded telepathically, his word soft and loving.

"Dominic?" I kissed his forehead, his cheeks, his lips. The corners of his mouth lifted slightly, but he didn't kiss me back. "Dominic, can you open your eyes?"

"*Only my mind to you, my love.*"

"Will you live?"

"*Long enough to kill Joshua.*" Though his response sounded tired, it was still edged in poison.

"You can't. *Damn.* You can't even be seen by him again. He'll know you're not normal."

Dominic's brows lifted slightly, but he still didn't open his eyes.

I kissed his lips again. "I didn't mean that like it sounded." I stroked his arm, then released his long hair from its leather strap and combed my fingers through the silky strands. "Would it help if I gave you some of my blood? Would it make you stronger?"

He didn't respond. I laid my head on his chest and listened to the faint beat of his heart. "I would have killed Joshua myself," I murmured against Dominic.

His hand swept over my back, but there was no strength in his touch. "*Stay away from him, Marissa.*"

"After what he did to you—"

"*I didn't react quickly enough to his spell. I've only just gained these warlock abilities myself, and I'm not used to calling on them to aid me. Besides, he's an advanced class warlock.*"

"But so are you!"

"*Yes, but as I said, I'm not used to having the ability. It takes time to remember the spells, to cast them, to react to those being cast. You aren't an advanced class witch, so stay away from him.*"

My back stiffened, and he attempted to calm me down by

rubbing it soothingly. But I wasn't in the mood to be placated. "What were you planning to do to Lynetta tonight?"

His thoughts remained silent.

"You can't do whatever you planned to, not the way you've been injured." When he didn't respond, I grumbled, "If you had done what I said and stayed in the kitchen, none of this would have happened."

"Are you saying you enjoyed his kiss?"

My ire instantly stoked, I sat up on the bed. His dark brown eyes glared at me, but I scowled back just as furiously. The very idea!

I shook my head. "If you don't get that jealousy under control, there will be nothing between us." Before he could reach out and stop me, I stood. "Get your rest. The pizza should be done any minute now. When you have your strength back, come join us."

"Marissa."

I couldn't stand his pleading one moment and saying hateful things the next. Wasn't I supposed to be happy he was alive again? I was. I just didn't care for these jealous fits he had. And I *really* didn't like his implication that I had enjoyed Joshua's kiss. How could Dominic think something like that after Joshua had nearly killed him?

"I'll...I'll see you later." I crossed the floor to the door, unlocked it and pulled it open. Kate held her hand up to the door, ready to strike at it, and I stifled a scream.

She smiled, her voice shaky. "Pizza's done. How's Dominic?"

Folding my arms, I simply said, "Ornery."

She glanced in the room. "That's good, isn't it?"

No, I didn't think so at all.

"If he's feeling...well, cantankerous, that means he's getting better," Kate said. "Mom always says that about Dad. First, you would think he was dying and he's the biggest baby when he's sick, and the next thing you know, he's an ogre, demanding and all."

"Right." I closed the door, and we headed down the stairs. "So how long have you been eavesdropping?"

Kate's eyes grew big, and she feigned hurt that I would think such a thing of her.

I yanked on a blond curl drifting over her shoulder. "How long?" I wasn't letting her get away with pretending she hadn't been spying.

"It seemed to be a one-sided conversation."

I smiled, glad that Kate hadn't heard too much, then.

"You know, you might want to lighten up on Dominic a bit. He can't help that he's so in love with you that he doesn't want other guys taking advantage of you. How would you have felt if Lynetta was kissing Dominic against his will?"

My hands fisted at my sides. "I would have wanted to kill her."

"Yes, exactly. So now you see how Dominic feels about you?"

I nodded, my stomach churning with guilt.

"So he had no choice, really."

"I just didn't want him getting hurt, or revealing what he truly was. What if Joshua had learned Dominic was a...Prince of Darkness?" I paused at the end of the hallway. "I'll tell him I'm sorry. Just serve the pizza, and I'll be down in a minute."

Kate wrapped her arm around me and hugged. "See you in a sec."

Thank goodness Kate was always, well, *almost always*, a pillar of wisdom when my emotions got the best of me.

I strode back to the bedroom, hoping Dominic wouldn't be too upset with my awful behavior. When I opened the door, my heart stopped dead.

The bed was empty.

15

D OMINIC

"I LOVE YOU, Marissa, with all my heart."

Whether she could understand the strong feelings I had for her or not, I had to destroy the vamp who threatened to condemn me to a life of darkness. Then I would destroy Joshua. But no matter what, I wanted to protect Marissa.

I had pretended weakness to throw her off, and I figured if I lived through my encounter with Lynetta, Marissa would kill me for being so deceitful. But how could I not? To stop me from harming myself this evening, I was certain she'd tie me to the bed if she could. Yet, I knew she would be furious with me once she discovered me missing.

I had no choice. Lynetta waited for me somewhere. Even now, I sensed her evil presence nearby. We had to play the game and end it now before the spiteful vampire killed Marissa. As jealous as I was of Joshua kissing Marissa, I knew Lynetta would even be more so of Marissa sharing her blood with me. And I now truly believed that's how my angel was my salvation—it was through her gift of her magic powers to me, not that she had to kill the vamp herself.

Instantly, I arrived at Lynetta's two-story brick home. She had thirty more homes all over the world. But I felt she would stick close to this one until she permanently had me under her control. There was no sign of her. Off feeding on the general populace, or coming for me, I assumed.

"Well," a feminine voice said behind me, sultry and sexy, "you've come home to Lynetta."

I turned to see the redheaded vamp, Karin, twisting a long curl around her slender finger. She was in her early twenties and had been a Baylor University student when Lynetta had caught hold of her. The newly turned vamp still attended classes, only now they were night classes.

"You seem kind of pale. Need a bit of blood to perk you up?" She ran her long red nail down her neck, leaving a streak of fresh blood. "Lynetta said you wouldn't feast on the general population like the rest of us have—which pleased her, since you were supposed to only feed off her to strengthen your union. But..." Karin cast a sinister smile, "feeding off that witch wasn't in the plans. So, you wanna little of my blood since you've already broken the rules?"

Puzzled, I lifted a brow. Lynetta would be in a foul mood if she learned I'd taken blood from one of her minions. So why was Karin making the proposal? Unless she figured Lynetta was tired of my messing with Marissa and had put me on her terminal list. Still, the sight of Karin's blood trickling down the cut she'd made stirred my bloodlust all over again. But I had to have Marissa's. No other. Bonding with her would keep me strong. Drinking anyone else's blood would dilute our connection, I was certain.

The vamp ran her hand through my hair. Her lips turned upward, and her green eyes smiled wickedly. "You seem tired. Not your venomous self."

I had been pretty outspoken amongst those Lynetta had turned. Furious to be one of them. Fighting being turned further. But now, I realized too late, my strength hadn't returned in full force. I was as weak as a newborn colt with barely the energy to stand on my own two feet. Apparently, I'd used the last of my reserves just getting here. I'd thought I was revived, but in truth, I had barely recovered from my injury.

I stepped back from her, intending to return to Marissa's loving touch and the safety and comfort of her home, to beg her forgiveness. But when I tried to return, I couldn't.

Dumbfounded, I just stood there. Then, panic-stricken, I wondered if I had really blown it this time.

"They're trying to find a way into her house," the vamp said. "So they can get you and bring you back here." She smiled. "Imagine, they haven't a clue that I have you all to myself." She touched my sleeve. "You seem so passive. Are you all right?"

I yanked my arm away from her. She smiled. Every weak move I made seemed to amuse her. She took another step forward. If I erased her mind…

But if I did that, would I use any strength I had built up and become weaker than I was now? No matter the cost, I had to find my way back to Marissa's house. As feeble as I was, I couldn't stay here in the devil's own home.

Maybe if I used a more conventional way I could do it. But before I could go, I would have to clear the vamp's mind. She obviously didn't want the others knowing she had me under her thumb at the moment, so she didn't convey my arrival telepathically to any others who might be close enough by to hear her.

I began to clear her mind, then stopped. "Does anyone who lives here have a vehicle?"

She snorted.

I guessed the answer was no and finished clearing her mind. Then I hurried out the front door into the dark where the other creatures of the night, such as me, lurked in the shadows. It already seemed like centuries ago that I had first seen Marissa and fallen in love.

I blew out my breath, deeply exasperated that I could barely stand. Just this once, I would try to return to my own home on foot. Knowing the other bloodsuckers watched my house to see if I would return there, I'd been avoiding it. But now they most likely focused their attention on Marissa's house. However, I was afraid I couldn't get close enough to attempt to shift into her place until I recovered somewhat. I would have to chance returning to my own. Maybe by morning, I would be recovered enough to return to Marissa's, yet the thought of leaving her alone all night didn't sit well with me.

Then I thought of my cell phone. I didn't know Marissa's number offhand, so I called home.

"Mom...mom..." I paused when my mother promptly burst into tears over the phone. I hated it when she cried, but especially when I needed their help so, and precious moments were ticking away.

"Hello?" James said, his voice forceful and worried.

Thank God my brother was there. "James, I need you to pick me up at Sanborn and Riverside. I'm on foot and I can't do my usual transportation, so I'm awfully vulnerable."

"I'm on my way." The phone clicked dead and at once, I felt cut off from humanity, left to wander alone in the darkness, hiding from Lynetta and her blood bonds.

Both my mother and father had fallen apart over my change, but thankfully, James had dealt with it much better. Maybe because of his youth. Or maybe because he was used to my shenanigans and getting me out of trouble. In any event, I was extremely glad James would drop everything to come to my aid.

For what seemed like hours, I waited, hidden in the shrubs next to a house only three blocks away from Lynetta's. Then I heard James's pickup engine grumbling a block away, sounding like music to my ears. The beaten and rusted, but most reliable piece of junk on wheels I could ever have wished for, appeared like a blue metal monster, creeping along the street while James kept an eye out for me.

He slowed the pickup only a few feet away, and I dashed out of the brush. I yanked open the creaking door and jumped into his cab, stumbling and nearly falling headlong into James.

"What's happening, Dominic?" James helped me back into the seat, then I managed to slam the door and he drove off.

He glanced at me, then kept his eyes focused on the road, his broad shoulders tense, his hazel eyes worried. I noticed then he'd gotten his hair cut shorter, more in a bur, and he'd added more of that lightening gel. If he didn't quit doing that, he would no longer look like my brother, but some beach dude from Southern California.

"Go east, to Whispering Oaks Estates," I ordered, concerned we still might get caught.

James turned the truck around and sped away from Lynetta's neighborhood while I explained my latest troubles. "I tried to kill the vamp but was struck by a warlock's spell tonight. I hadn't realized how weak it made me."

"How in the hell did you get mixed up with a warlock?" Again, he glanced at me, his eyes narrowed in condemnation. "Jeez, Dominic, you look like hell."

"Thanks," I mumbled, not feeling in the best of health either. "Lightning bolt spells will do that to a body."

James shook his head. "I don't even want to know how that

came about. I thought you said you couldn't go against the vampire. You said—"

"Things have changed. I've met a girl."

James glanced at me, a slight smile curving his lips. As many times as I got into trouble with some girl—who hadn't quite ditched her old boyfriend—James would teasingly call me Lover Boy. Would I ever learn?

Lynetta taught me the lesson well to avoid most girls. Marissa was definitely the exception.

"Marissa's a witch." I knew that would get mixed reviews.

Frowning, James shook his head. "Okay, so that explains the warlock. You sure know how to get yourself into messes. What in the world are you taking up with a witch for when you've got a vampire after you?"

"Marissa saved my life. She's *saving* my life. I've found my soul mate."

James grunted. He wouldn't believe in such a thing unless someone cast a spell on him, forcing him to believe it.

"Really." I'm sure he thought I was an idiot with foolish romantic notions. "We can read each other's minds."

This time James looked at me with a kind of amazement.

"She's truly the one. If she can't help me, no one can."

"Soooo, where is this girl when you need her help so badly?" Though disbelief still clung to his words, I also sensed some hope.

"Lynetta's threatened her. I was afraid for Marissa's safety. I thought once I had warlock powers..."

James glanced at me and raised his brows. "You *know, I'm* the eldest and *I'm* supposed to be the one who tries lots of new experiences out first. *You're* supposed to follow my lead and not make the same dumb mistakes I make. So what's wrong with this scenario?"

"You're the eldest and supposed to be more responsible. I'm the youngest and…" I shrugged. What else could I say? I was rash, impulsive, didn't have a whole lot of common sense—that's what Dad said as soon as I told my parents what had happened to me. "Well, anyway, Marissa gave me some of her blood. I didn't realize I'd gain a warlock's abilities when I drank her blood, but I did."

"Warlock's abilities?" He shook his head. "Jeez, Mom and Dad will throw a fit. You know neither of them had gray hair until you turned seventeen."

I rolled my eyes. "They said they turned gray prematurely because it was an inherited trait."

"They only said that so you wouldn't feel so bad. What else is going on?"

Wringing my damp hands, I stared out the window. "I thought I would be stronger and could kill the vamp. Except a warlock attempted to murder me first."

The whites of James's knuckles showed when he gripped the steering wheel tightly. "The lightning bolt spell." He attempted to give me a sympathetic look, but there was a strong undercurrent of anger, and I knew if I gave him the warlock's name, James would try to take care of the bastard himself. "How was the warlock involved?"

"He made a move on Marissa."

James's brown brows rose in question.

"He forced a kiss on her, but I know it was to rile me. I really tried to remain calm, but when I came after him, he cast the spell on me."

"Who is he and where is he now?"

"I don't know." I told the truth in part. I had no idea where the warlock had gone, though I suspected his home, but even then, I didn't know where. I knew his first name, but not his last. So my answer was mostly the truth.

"You do, but you won't tell me." James took a deep breath. "I suspect you don't want to go home."

"No, I'm staying with Marissa. I have to protect her, and I need her help. Plus, I don't think Mom and Dad can take much more of what's going on in my life without both of them having a stroke."

"Hell, Dominic, you're going to give *me* a stroke if you keep it up." James glanced at me. "Where does she live?"

"Whispering Oaks Estates."

James's eyes widened. "She has her own house? How old *is* this girl?"

"Seventeen. Her parents are away."

James chuckled, all knowing-like.

"We haven't...well, first things first."

Shaking his head, James said, "Her address?"

"Thirty-two-ten Lake Vista Drive. Can you tell Mom we're working on clearing this matter up? I want to keep in touch, but every time I call—"

"She's scared to death about you. And now with all of these killings..."

Knowing how hard it must be for her, I sighed deeply. "I haven't done any of them."

"I know. But still she's worried you'll begin to also."

"I have to break the spell by Friday." With the setback tonight, I wasn't sure we would make it in time, yet I had to keep my hopes up. A residual of the lightning bolt spell zapping my strength was making me feel impotent. The thought of Marissa hating me for leaving her like I did also weighed heavily on my conscience. I was certain I would have to face her fury next, and I wasn't sure I could handle it.

James tapped on the steering wheel with his thumbs. "Is there anything I can do?"

"Listen, you were absolutely a lifesaver tonight. Wait, pull over here. I can't get into the house without transporting, but it's only a block away, and I'm afraid Lynetta might be hanging around outside trying to get in. Let me try from here."

James stopped at the curb. "We're all rooting for you, little brother."

"I have to tell you, Marissa's got a girlfriend who's a pretty hot number, and she's interested in meeting you."

James slid his hands over the steering wheel. "Don't tell me. She's a witch."

"Yep. Of course she was disappointed you weren't more like me."

James laughed out loud.

I patted him on the shoulder. "It's good to hear you laugh like that again. I didn't think I ever would."

"It's good to see you still alive and well, grayer than our cement walk, but still kicking."

"As soon as I can, I'll give you the news about how we make out."

"If everything turns out well..." James stopped, his voice breaking up. "You'll have to bring this little filly home to see Mom and Dad."

"Will do. I hope they won't be too upset that I'm a warlock now...or that she's a witch."

James snorted. "I think anything would be preferable to a—"

"Prince of Darkness."

16

M ARISSA

MY HEART and head pounded with frustration and worry while I rushed out of my parents' house with Kate, not knowing where to go to save Dominic from himself.

Neither of us felt assured that he was indeed totally revived from his lightning bolt experience. Unless he'd only faked his loss of strength. Then I would kill him for lying to me once I got my hands on him.

But why didn't he wait until after we'd fallen asleep? Why the ruse? Because I'd been so angry with him, I made him leave.

To have him home safely, I would take every word and action back.

"To the Hamburger Spot?" I asked Kate, my voice verging on panic. "That's where he said he met Lynetta the first time. Do you think he'll try meeting her there again?"

Kate agreed. "I have no other idea where he might go. Sounds good to me."

Before we could move but a few feet from the house, a breeze suddenly stirred, and a flapping of wings clued us in to a vampire's arrival. At once my heart sank, filling with black dread.

Lynetta sneered at me from several paces away. Dressed in tight-fitting, black leather pants and a short-waisted jacket, she looked like a biker babe who'd lost her wheels. Her long, black hair hung to her hips in thick, luscious curls. Again, her soulless, raven-colored eyes glared at me. With her wicked fangs hidden, I could see now that she was a beauty.

"Stupid little witch," she hissed.

Instantly, she destroyed the image I had of her being a beauty.

Hoping they would work against a powerful ancient vampire, both Kate and I hastily formed protection spells around us.

"Dominic wanted you as a midnight snack," the vamp taunted. "That's what he told me. But nooooo, then he decided he wanted to keep you for his very own plaything."

Her voice was dark and sultry with a charming lure to it. But I couldn't believe the vamp twisted the story around so. Did she believe we would think she was telling the truth? After what she'd nearly done to him in front of me? Why didn't she just attack us and be done with it?

"He said I was to play this little charade of his. He would follow you to your house, then try to solicit your help to get rid of me. Except you balked at letting him in. Must have killed his superior self-image. Ancients have egos as big as the world, you know."

"You stalked him at the Hamburger Spot," I countered,

knowing she lied. No way had he come after me to pretend to get rid of Lynetta as part of some sadistic game.

"The other way around, sweetie." Lynetta gave a sickly-sweet, all-knowing smile. "He likes young things, you see. He shows up where the teens hang out." She barely took a breath and rattled on. "He commanded me to perform and staged the entire scene. He's the one who turned me...not the other way around. He's the ancient one, not me. Since he turned me, I have no choice but to do his bidding. Believe me, I hate you because I want him all to myself, but..." She lifted one shoulder in a defeated shrug. "He's the one in charge. You were the ultimate challenge, don't you see? A witch who could not easily be compelled to do his bidding. That's why he found you so...intriguing. He tired of human females he could control just by gazing into their eyes."

I quickly considered what had happened as far as I remembered it, though the vamp was screwing with my memories. Had he targeted me in the manner she said? Easily winning me over by soliciting my aid in his defense? Inviting a stranger into my home when I would not normally have?

Squashing my doubts, I said through clenched teeth, "He didn't change you. He can be out during the daylight hours. You can't. You're the one who's the ancient vampire. You're the one who turned him."

"Did he tell you I couldn't be outside during the day?" Her laughter was bitter, cutting through me like scissors ripped through silk. "Did he tell you also if you share your blood with him, and his with you, then kill me, all will be well? That he has a family around here somewhere? Have you met them? They died three hundred and fifty years ago, after he ripped their throats out. He had an older brother. Has he told you that?"

I glanced at Kate. Her eyes were as round as the full moon.

"His older brother would have inherited the dukedom.

Dominic would have had nothing, being the youngest son. He killed his family when his father was sick and dying."

Lynetta folded her arms. "As to the business of daylight, he has always been able to move around during the day, as long as it's sufficiently overcast. Didn't he tell you that? We all are."

"I don't believe you." Yet a trickle of dread dared to shimmer down my spine. What if what she said was the truth?

"He wants you to kill me now, doesn't he? I was to be his mistress for all eternity. He'll promise you the same. Immortality. And after a month or so, he'll find some new girl to hit on. But do you know *why* he wanted you?"

Truthfully, I couldn't think of a reason. There had to be millions of girls who were prettier, more athletic, brighter, wittier, you name it. Any of them would beat me out.

"You're a witch. And not just any witch, but plain to look at, gullible and never been kissed. So you were vulnerable to a vampire's charms like the kind Dominic possesses. He has all the women swooning at his feet. In essence, you were ripe for the picking."

My heart quickened. I could think all of these things about myself. I often did, but some vamp wasn't going to say them about me. Still, I wondered how she knew I'd never been kissed. Was it written on my lips? Had she guessed? Or worse, had Dominic told her?

"You're the ancient one, Lynetta," I said as calmly as I could manage, though my blood raced through my system and my cheeks grew hot with anger.

Still keeping her canines tucked away, she smiled in a sort of simpering sympathetic way as if she felt sorry for me. "At first, I wanted to kill you, because I wanted to be Dominic's only mistress. You can't understand how his betrayal has ripped out my heart. To prove he is the ancient vampire, I'll not harm you or your friend. It's not your fault he has played with your heart-strings and wrapped you around his will."

She waved a finger at me. "Did he have a difficult time stopping when he drank your blood? If not the last time, he will this time. Mark my words."

Lynetta twisted everything. I kept telling myself she was the one who had turned Dominic, not the other way around. Yet, a niggling fear worked its way into my subconscious, setting up self-doubt that promised to plague me until I knew the whole truth.

"Dominic hasn't fully turned you. But he already told you that you are soul mates, has he not? He said the same to me. Now he says that if you don't kill me, I will fully turn him. Am I right? If I fully turn him, he'll come for you no matter what. Right? Whether it was your choice or not? He's preparing you for what he'll do, as he did me. You tell him no, that he can't have your blood. See what happens. He'll beg you to give it to him. When that doesn't work, he'll take what he has claimed. If he were the good guy in all this, he wouldn't do such a thing, would he?"

"Why would he have us kill you then, if you're not the ancient vampire? Why not just let you roam free to find someone else?" I felt very clever for an instant—even a bit smug.

"He knows how bitter I am about his betrayal. He's afraid I'll turn his potential victims against him. I can't kill him because he turned me, but I could get others to go after him. Now he has taken your witch's blood and become even more powerful." The last words Lynetta spoke seemed somewhat angered, but she attempted to maintain an even voice—non-threatening—to convince me she was the innocent in this situation. "He'll continue to feast on the population here until it gets too risky, then move somewhere else. But he'll keep you around for a while. See if he can tap into any more of your abilities. Once he's finished using you, he'll solicit the help of someone else to kill you like he plans to do to me."

She took a step toward me, but Kate and I stood our ground, hoping to heaven our protection spell would last, but not wanting to cower before the spiteful vamp. "Remember my words well, witch. He intended to kill me tonight, but I hid from his deadly fangs. He'll ask for your help again, beg for you to aid him, or he'll be lost to the dark side." Lynetta spit on the ground. "He *is* the dark side. Help him and you'll join him, too, for a time."

With a flick of her wrist, faux biker babe Lynetta vanished.

My legs shook, and Kate grabbed my arm. We hurried back to my front porch. "She lied," I sobbed, not sure why I suddenly didn't trust Dominic. Yet my faith in him was shaken. I couldn't help wondering why he had selected me? Plain old me? None of the guys had ever paid any attention to me. I wasn't outgoing or spectacular in any way. Had Lynetta spoken the truth?

"Why are you crying then?" Kate closed and locked the front door.

"I keep wondering why he picked me. Out of all the beautiful people, why did he choose plain old brown-paper-bag me?"

"Because you're beautiful to me," Dominic's deep voice said behind us from the direction of the living room sofa.

Kate squealed and I gasped. We whirled around to see him gripping the sofa back, his face pale as death, his dark brown eyes haunted.

"You're more beautiful than anyone, Marissa," he repeated as if trying to convince me he spoke the truth. He turned his attention to Kate. "Can we be alone?"

"No." I grabbed Kate's hand, tired and determined not to be conned by any more vampires. "It's...it's time for bed, and we'll see you in the morning."

"Marissa, I love you."

I nodded. Any words I might have said to him clung in my throat like a chunk of lead.

His face was still ice white, but his knuckles reddened from the fierce grip he had on the sofa. Was he angry with me?

Suddenly, he collapsed on the floor. Kate shrieked, shattering my already raw nerves, while my heart took a dive.

The night hadn't gone well at all. Dominic was in bad physical shape, I was an emotional wreck, and Kate wasn't much better. After many hours of sitting with Dominic while he stretched out on the couch unconscious, I finally carried him to the guest bedroom. Kate followed like a little lost lamb.

While she watched me silently for a few minutes, I kept hoping she would go to bed. Then she finally whispered, "I'll see you in the morning."

I nodded, not wanting to tell her what I was going to do, but she seemed to know anyway.

She padded down the hall to my bedroom with slow, weary steps and shut the door. At first, I removed Dominic's shoes and socks. I stared at his trousers for what seemed an eternity, the thought crossing my mind that I'd imagined him stripped naked and put on display by the witch's tribunal. Seemed like an eternity had passed since we'd first met.

I unbuckled his belt and unzipped his trousers. Well, I wouldn't strip him totally, just enough so he could sleep comfortably.

I tugged at his pants for some time, then finally pulled them off and landed on my butt for the third time that day. I squashed the swear word that rose to my lips.

Next, I worked on his shirt, then pulled it off. He muttered under his breath, though his pulse was still weak. He hadn't regained consciousness since he had collapsed in the living room, which had me worried sufficiently to fear I might still lose him. I held back more tears. I'd shed enough already. For now, I had work to do to keep him alive.

Where had he gone, and what had he done while he was away? He hadn't been seeing Lynetta because the vamp was harassing me. So what had happened to him? I was dying to know and to tell him all that Lynetta had said. I had to know his version of the story, again, to reassure me that he had told the truth. Though I didn't think for an instant he was faking his weakness now, and if he wasn't pretending, how could he be an ancient vampire?

I slipped my shoes and pants off. Wearing only a silky blouse and panties, I climbed under the covers with him, and rested my head on his chest. For being half dead, he surprised me when his hand wrapped around my waist and pulled me closer.

If he had indeed been the ancient vampire as Lynetta had claimed, I decided it didn't matter. He'd charmed me right into loving him, and I wanted him, even if only briefly. It was better than not ever being wanted at all.

At least that's what I figured. My mind warred with my heart though, tugging my thoughts this way and that. The notion anyone would use me for his or her own personal gain hurt my pride.

For an instant, he held me close, then the effort seemed to weary him, and my heart reached out to him, striking down my feeble doubts. "Dominic," I whispered against his ear, "do you need some of my blood to strengthen you?"

His eyelids fluttered opened, and I assumed that meant yes. Again, I was slightly apprehensive. It seemed like eons since the last time he'd taken my blood.

Would it hurt this time? Would he stop when he had his fill before he took too much of my own, or would he have difficulty like Lynetta had said?

I pulled my hair aside for him and offered my throat. He

didn't move toward me, just studied me with his liquid, chocolate eyes that had a sad, faraway look. At first, I was crushed. Then I vacillated between worrying he no longer wanted me and concern that he was too weak even to feed. I couldn't see mutilating myself to offer my blood if he couldn't have it any other way. In fact, having my blood drawn had always made me squeamish, to the extent I'd passed out when the dermatologist removed a suspicious-looking mole on my shoulder the year before. I shuddered just thinking about offering him my blood.

"Dominic? Can you hear me?"

He continued to watch me but didn't respond. I leaned forward and kissed his lips gently at first. Maybe this was how we needed to do it—like we had done the previous night. Much more pleasant to think about kissing than giving blood.

He kissed me back, his tongue pressing to part my lips. He seemed to have regained his appetite, except I worried whether he desired more than my blood at the moment. He slid his hands over my back, the silky shirt slipping around.

"Marissa."

"Dominic, are you going to be all—"

His lips pressed hard against mine, passionately, enthusiastically desperate. I matched his kiss, feeling the same kind of fiery desperation.

My molecules bumped and crashed while electricity zinged through my insides.

Breathlessly, he whispered against my cheek, "Stop me if I hurt you. Don't ever let me hurt you."

Hearing his words, despite the lack of strength they contained, cheered my heart. Again, I brushed my hair aside and exposed my throat. I desired the intimate bond that made us one when he drank my blood, the ecstasy that filled me with pleasure when he sucked away.

Suddenly a floorboard under the carpet squeaked next to

the bedroom door, alerting us of someone's untimely and most unwelcome presence. My first thought was that it was Kate, unable to sleep, worried about Dominic.

When I twisted my head to look at the doorway, the evil warlock, Joshua, stood tall, his black eyes narrowed, his dark hair disheveled as if he'd just fallen out of bed—on the wrong side.

My heart lurched in panic.

"He doesn't deserve you, Marissa," Joshua said, a mocking smile on his thin, pale lips. "Let me do the honors."

17

D OMINIC

I COULDN'T BELIEVE my awful luck—me a Prince of Darkness, and an utter failure at that. The love of my life was shortly to become the meal of the warlock she'd had a crush on, who didn't care one ounce about her, and I had no strength to save her.

"Marissa, if you and Kate and I can hit him with a lightning bolt, we can temporarily drain the strength from him," I telepathically communicated to her, realizing now Joshua had to be a minion of Lynetta, furious with myself for not figuring it out before. He could let the vamp and more of her blood bonds into Marissa's house at any time, and we would all be doomed.

"You're too weak, Dominic," she said, holding my hand in a crushing grip. Her body trembled slightly, making me feel worse.

I tried to hide the look of shame that must have crossed my face.

She lessened the grip on my hand, maybe sensing how powerful her physical strength had become. *"You are not a failure, Dominic! But I can't reach Kate with my thoughts, and I doubt Joshua will allow me to physically go to her. If he knew what we were going to attempt to do to him—"*

"He won't believe you're capable of doing such a thing to him, as sweet as you are."

She didn't say anything in response, but I could tell she didn't believe me.

"And he knows I'm too weak to attempt it on my own," I continued, ignoring her implication that she didn't think she was always sweet. I knew better—even when she was mad, she had good reason to be. Her actions were never calculated or mean, not like Lynetta's.

"Damn you, Joshua!" Marissa suddenly shouted, loud enough to wake up the whole household—if there had been anyone there but Kate and us.

Joshua smiled—a look that was pure malevolence. "If you are attempting to wake Kate, she's asleep. Worn out by the amount of blood I already drained from her."

Marissa paled, tears misted her eyes, and she held her stomach. I worried she was going to be sick all over the bed. This definitely wasn't good news, and I couldn't help feeling once again that I'd totally screwed up. If I hadn't tried to chase Lynetta down, I would have more strength to face this devil now.

"Don't worry, dear Marissa," Joshua continued, though his tone was menacing, not comforting. "Kate will be fine in the morning. Be assured, I didn't drink enough of her blood to deter me from wanting yours, too."

Marissa's back stiffened and she climbed out of bed. Her shirt covered her panties, but Joshua still took in his fill of her as if she stood naked before him. I felt totally useless, my body weak and unable to respond to the warlock's blatant actions, though rage burned inside me, and I wanted to smash his head with my fist.

Then Marissa began to say strange words in her head, words I couldn't comprehend, nor could I catch the way she spoke them. Then finally they caught hold in my mind. *"Felshion, Carpathian, Rasmussin, Lorengi, Aqua, Killon!"*

I repeated her words silently while she chanted them again, though I had no earthly idea what she was up to. The words seemed slightly familiar, but I couldn't dredge up the elusive memory of where I'd heard them before. I definitely couldn't twist my thoughts around them the way she did, as if she had spoken the exotic foreign language all her life and I couldn't master it. Yet I knew from the desperation and determination in her voice that she had a plan, the only one we had at the moment, and I wanted badly to know what it was.

The third time she spoke the chant was the charm. The water entity appeared. The one Marissa had conjured up on stage. The one her teacher said didn't count as a spell. And then it dawned on me. I'd seen something like this when I was in elementary school. A water demon. At least I presumed that's what she was from pictures I'd seen of the elusive creatures in a book about stranger-than-fiction entities, though never had I seen one in the flesh, well, *water*, before. Seeing her in Marissa's memories didn't count.

In robes of aqua silk—liquid like her face—and long blue curls dripping down her hips, the demon moved fluidly, her actions mesmerizing.

Again, Marissa began to chant, only this time verbally, her words strong, commanding. "Aqua, Killon, Sleuthing, Hellion, Racine."

I repeated her words, and then Kate did from the hallway, too, her voice raspy and weak.

My heart lifted to see Kate, her face pale, almost as colorless as the long white T-shirt she wore. Marissa gave Kate a half smile. But she quickly turned her full attention on the demon and motioned toward Joshua, who was frozen by the demon's appearance. And Marissa thought she wasn't good at spells? I hrumpfed deep inside. My lifemate was a bundle of contradictions. I'd never heard of a witch or warlock being able to summon any kind of demon.

The demon's sculptured face remained emotionless when she wrapped her arms around Joshua, who stood spellbound. Enraptured with her beauty? Or so scared he couldn't move? I would never know the reason, I figured, nor did it truly matter as long as the demon aided us when we very much needed some kind of intervention on our behalf.

The demon sucked the water from Joshua's body, drawing it out like streams of blue mist, pulling it into her own watery form. After several seconds, Joshua collapsed on the floor. His dehydrated skin was drawn tightly over bones, his eyes shut tight, his face emotionless. He was no longer a menace—for the moment, at least.

Marissa began to chant again. I lay my head back on the pillow, exhausted, unable to follow the words she spoke this time. I heard her say only "the Gulf of Mexico", and I assumed she told the demon to return to her watery habitat. Just as quickly as the demon had appeared, the fluid blue figure vanished in a whirlpool spin.

Dashing to Kate, Marissa wrapped her arms around her. "Are you all right, Kate?"

"All your yelling woke me up," Kate groused, half teasing, her words weary.

Marissa smiled and hugged her friend. Selfishly, I wished she'd embraced me in the same manner.

"What are we to do with Joshua?" Kate asked, holding her hand over the puncture wounds on her throat.

"Kill him," I said, without a bit of hesitation.

The two girls looked at me as if I meant only to seek vengeance. Yet for all he had done, couldn't they see how dangerous he was to all of us?

"If he hasn't already, he can let Lynetta in," I explained, not appreciating that the girls wouldn't jump to agree with me. That's all the convincing I would have needed, if I were them, I thought. I didn't stop there, afraid they still hadn't gotten the point. "Not only that, but he's targeted Kate, too. And you, Marissa. He'll kill me once he has a chance, also."

Marissa nodded, though I could tell she didn't like the idea of destroying a fellow warlock she'd known for years. The part that really gave me a kick in the gut was that she'd had a crush on him. Did she still?

She looked over at me, her blue eyes wide. "No, Dominic. I only care for you."

"I have an idea," Kate said, leaning against Marissa for support. "My Aunt Zoe owns the Sexy Nail shop."

Wordlessly, I stared at her, wondering if Kate had lost some of her marbles when she'd given too much blood. Now wasn't the time to get a manicure.

Kate continued to speak, her voice still raspy, totally winded. "It's connected to a tanning bed salon. An unlocked doorway leads from one part of the building to the other. My aunt's friend runs the tanning salon, and they watch each other's businesses so they both don't have to be there all the time."

I still wasn't getting her drift.

Kate frowned at me, I guess perturbed because I looked so

puzzled. "The tanning bed uses ultraviolet light to burn its victims," she further explained, her voice exasperated.

Instantly getting her point, I smiled. But how were we going to get there?

"I'll drive the car," Marissa quickly offered.

"I have a key to the place because I give manicures sometimes to help my aunt out," Kate said.

I shook my head, then climbed out of bed. "You can't go alone, Marissa. I'll go with you."

Kate immediately focused on my boxers embossed with shiny red lips and she gave a muffled giggle.

I frowned at her.

"The water demon's work on Joshua should last until morning, but I think moving him out of the house tonight is the only choice we have," Marissa said, her words spoken quickly as if she wanted to get this done now, and I couldn't have agreed more. "Kate, do you really think you're up to coming with us?"

I felt the same way about Kate's condition, though I wasn't much better off.

"I feel awfully lightheaded and tired, but I don't want to be left alone."

After what had happened, I could definitely understand her reluctance to be left alone here. I wondered though, why Joshua hadn't let Lynetta or the others into Marissa's house. Did he want a go at Marissa first and figured he wouldn't have a chance once Lynetta got a hold of her? He would have been right.

"All right. Go get dressed, and so will we. I'll come for you in half an hour, and then we'll go to your aunt's nail shop," Marissa said, all businesslike, as if we were going to the movies and the show was about to begin.

She closed and locked the door while Kate walked back to Marissa's bedroom.

"First," Marissa said, taking complete command, walking back to the bed, "you need to have a little dessert."

I grinned at her, totally agreeable. "I like it when you take charge, Marissa."

"Yeah, I bet you say that to all the girls."

I wiggled my brows, amused at her comment. "Not me."

"The more fun for me, then." Then her brows knit in a frown. "Yeah, except for the last time when I told you not to tackle Lynetta on your own and you didn't listen to me."

She really had me there. I shrugged. "Remember what Kate said. It's a guy thing."

An elusive smile touched her lips. After climbing into bed beside me, she leaned over and kissed my mouth lightly, as if I would break.

She felt soft and cuddly, and I ran my fingers through her satiny blond hair. "I don't understand how you can think I wouldn't love you like I do."

"Shh," she said, holding her finger to my lips.

I captured her hand and sucked her finger. "Every bit of you is tasty."

Raising her brows, she gave me a look of teasing disbelief. "You're probably just starving."

"I am. I told you earlier I was."

"Yeah, and you didn't even get a bite of pizza either."

"Did you?"

Shaking her head, Marissa leaned down and kissed my lips. She nipped at my lower one, then sucked, stirring my blood to the nth degree.

Running my fingers over her throat, I felt the blood pulsing through her veins, beckoning to me. She stretched out her neck. "Go ahead, my prince. Bite me."

I grinned, then tangled my tongue freely with hers. I nuzzled her cheek and moved lower, her breath becoming shallow in anticipation. My canines had extended before I even realized, and when I dipped them into her skin, she gasped slightly.

I attempted to pull back, but again, she held me tight. *"Don't stop, Dominic. It only scares me for a minute, then the pleasure washes over me like a warm wave."*

I sucked her blood, the sweet liquid filling me with desire. I longed to make her my own in every way. My mate forever. The whole time, I stroked her arm, or her back, or raked my fingers through her gold hair. She rested underneath me, quietly, her eyes shut, her hands lying at her sides. Any movement on her part would cause her to tense and the blood withdrawal to pain her.

Finally, I pulled away, feeling stronger than ever before. I kissed her lips. She opened her eyes. "You didn't beg me to give my blood to you."

"I wouldn't have, Marissa. We're soul mates. You would have offered, and if you had not, I wouldn't have forced you to give me your blood. You always have to be willing, or I would be no better than him." I pointed at Joshua's wizened figure, a crumpled heap of dried skin stretched over bones and covered in baggy clothes on the bedroom floor.

I stared at the remains, then turned to Marissa, still awed by her incredible talent. "How did you know to call up a water demon?"

"I'm not that talented. She's my patron demon."

I lifted a brow, not understanding. I'd never heard of such a thing.

"You might have noticed how blue my eyes are."

I nodded. Her entrancing eyes had caught mine the first time I saw her. "Your eyes are beautiful—they enchanted me right away."

Her brows pinched in a thoughtful frown. "You're not an Aquarius, are you?"

"Yep, that's me." Though except for knowing the symbol and that my birth stone was amethyst, I didn't really know much else about the zodiac sign, and her bringing it up like she did intrigued me.

"Hmm, I thought you were. That's what my dad is. I imagine the fact you were born under the water-bearer sign is probably why my patron demon likes you, lucky for you. Did you know Aquarians are thought to be generous humanitarians, honest and loyal, inventive, very bright, and independent?"

I puffed up my chest, appreciating the sign's positive personality traits. Sounded just like me.

"On the darker side," she warned, a hint of sparkle in her eyes, "they can be contrary, perverse, unpredictable, detached, and unemotional."

"*Can be* are the catchwords. Certainly not me." I smiled when her lips curved up.

She pointed to the puddle on the floor left by the demon. "Very rarely does a witch or warlock have a patron demon. I was born on a fishing boat on the Gulf. A tropical storm nearly sank our boat, and my mother, in all her fright, delivered me early. The storm passed and the swells calmed. My father held me up to the water and praised the demon for taking care of us.

"The demon rose from the water and studied my blue eyes, and they, being the same color as hers, pleased her. She whispered the chant I spoke in the room. Since then, she has been my patron demon. I called her to join me at my seventeenth birthday celebration. She spun off waterspouts and we played in their spray." Marissa grinned at me and touched my cheek with her fingertips. "She wondered why a warlock was saying the chant also. But then she assumed we were bonded together as mates."

"We are. Though at the time, I thought you needed my help."

Marissa giggled. "Always."

Someone knocked on the door. "Are you guys decent yet?" Kate called out, her voice still sounding groggy.

"Just a minute!" Marissa yelled back in a panicked tone.

"Yeah, just as I suspected. I almost fell asleep waiting for you guys," Kate grumbled.

As soon as Marissa and I were dressed, I lifted Joshua off the floor. Luckily, Marissa's blood had rejuvenated me, and Joshua weighed no more than skin and bones. We hurried down the stairs, past the living room and into the kitchen.

Before we reached the door to the garage through the kitchen, we heard a key in the front door lock. As it twisted, metal grinding against metal, all of us froze.

Marissa grabbed my arm, and Kate seized the other as if I could protect all of us. I stood in the middle of the two girls holding the mummified-looking form of Joshua, wondering who was breaking into Marissa's house—with a key—and what we were to do next.

18

M ARISSA

WOULD a vampire seek to enter my parents' home using a key? Mom and Dad weren't due to come home until Friday. No way could it be them.

"Shit," my mother said, totally unlike her. I knew something was really wrong for her to be swearing on top of being home from their vacation two days early. I guessed they'd gotten a taxi to drive them home or I would hear my aunt's chatty voice about now. The situation was as strange a scenario as me standing next to one weary, but live vampire, carrying one half-dead vampire, who stood beside my blood-drained, extremely weakened girlfriend.

Something clanked against the tile entryway floor. But, as if Medusa had turned her gaze upon us and changed us all into stone statues, none of us could move. Thank God my mother couldn't see us from where she stood.

"Damn," my father groaned, his voice huskier than normal and full of pain. Then he rushed down the hall, slamming the door to the downstairs half bath.

"Make it to the toilet this time, will you, dear?" my mother called after him. "Damn tainted food. Ruin a good vacation every time," she mumbled. Then the front door banged shut and the lock clicked.

Finally breaking free of the spell, I wheeled around and opened the door to the garage for Kate and Dominic, who still cradled the wizened-up form of Joshua in his arms. We all hurried out to the Ford Taurus, then I poked the opener to the garage door and cringed when the metal groaned, creaking its displeasure all the way.

"Jeez, I hope they don't hear us leaving," I whispered, then turned to Kate who opted to sit in the front seat with me while Dominic sat in back with Joshua. "Did you shut my bedroom door?" I asked her.

She shook her head. "No need to."

My heart took a dive. "My mother will look in on me and find I'm not there. If the door's shut, she'll assume I'm tucked away in bed like I should be at this hour and won't bother to disturb me. Then when she discovers I'm not there, they'll find the car gone and call the police."

"Wait for me," Dominic said.

Before I could object, he vanished, and the moisture in my throat evaporated, too. I couldn't help worrying that Mom would catch him. What a disaster. The scenario would be slightly different then, but the final result the same. A call to the police.

After a few minutes of trying to control my rapid heartbeat, I gave a jump when Dominic finally reappeared in the back seat of the car. "Bedroom door is locked. If they try it, they'll think you're sleeping soundly."

Then a new worry began to nag at me. "What about the guest bedroom?"

Dominic stared at me, his look blank.

I bit back a curse, knowing any second we could get caught, knowing, too, there was no talking our way out of this one. My parents would *never* leave me home alone again, though I couldn't blame them. "The door is always shut, but I'm afraid if she looks in, she'll see there's a puddle of water on the carpet and the bed is a mess—if the open door doesn't create enough intrigue."

"Be back in a jif."

Hoping he wouldn't get caught, I took a deep, settling breath. It was bad enough Kate and I wouldn't be home, the car would be gone, and we had a wizened-up form of Joshua in the backseat, but if my parents caught sight of a gorgeous guy popping in and out of the bedrooms...

I rubbed my temple. The anxiety pooled into my brain, giving me one splitting headache. Or maybe some of it was from Dominic's feeding off me. I turned to Kate. "Are you okay?"

She nodded and leaned her head back against the headrest. "I was half asleep when he pounced on me. I feel no remorse for having to do what we have to with him. He hurt me, Marissa. Does it hurt with you and Dominic?"

"No, but he's gentle and warned me if I tensed it could hurt."

"Well, I tensed all right. Getting me to relax was not uppermost on Joshua's mind."

I touched Kate's neck where he'd left two bloody gashes. My stomach revolted. I jerked open the car's console, then pulled out a large-sized bandage from our emergency first-aid kit.

"Okay," Dominic said from the back seat, nearly making my heart leap out of my chest.

I finished bandaging Kate's neck, relieved that Joshua hadn't killed her. How would she explain the bite marks to her parents?

Then I drove down the driveway as quietly as I could, and shut the garage door, hoping that the grinding monstrosity wouldn't alert my parents. I headed into town toward Kate's aunt's shop, praying we wouldn't have any further problems tonight.

With the utmost caution, I drove the speed limit, obeying all the traffic rules, terrified we might get stopped by a policeman for some minor infraction.

By the time we arrived at the shop fifteen minutes later, both Dominic and Kate were sound asleep. I shook my head, wishing I hadn't had to take them with me as worn out as they were, but knowing I couldn't have left them behind at the house. What if my parents had discovered them?

After fumbling around in Kate's purse for what seemed an eternity, I found the key. First, I would unlock the door to the building. Then I would sneak Joshua in. Seemed like some grade B horror movie where none of the actors were well-known or good at their job. I was the main character, and all my accomplices had abandoned me.

I shuddered every time a car passed down the street. Half hidden in the dim lights of the buildings closed for the night, I hoped no one would notice me. I wished fervently that there had been a back door for my clandestine operations. What if someone saw me carrying a body into the building?

I had never even considered that.

But another anxiety wormed its way under my skin. What if one of Lynetta's minions caught us?

Finally, I managed to unlock the metal door and shove it open. Afterwards, I hurried back to the car, my tennis shoes slapping the asphalt like a warning bell, announcing to any vampire in the area I was out and about: "Come get me."

Neither Kate nor Dominic stirred when I opened the rear car door, and truthfully, I was relieved in part that they rested comfortably, knowing they needed sleep much more than me. But part of me hated that I had to do this alone, and anxiety gripped me like a boa constrictor. I couldn't shake loose of the feeling, no matter how much I tried to use the calming spell on my mind. I pulled the remains of Joshua from the backseat, then locked the car doors, figuring it would be easy enough to destroy his body without anyone else's help.

Already perspiration trickled between my breasts and down my forehead, despite how cool it was at this ungodly hour of the morning, the mist cloaking the darkness in a gray shroud.

Within seconds, I was inside the tanning salon, the front door shut and locked, and my heart pounding as fast as if I'd run a marathon.

I carried Joshua into one of the rooms. A stand-up shower stall faced me. I thought a lie-down, coffin-type would work better. Did she have one of those?

I'd never been into the tanning ritual thing. My fair skin went from white to blistered anytime I'd tried to get a tan, and consequently I had given up on the notion early on in my life. Like when I was about ten or so.

I hurried to the final room at the end of the hall, my last hope. I peered inside—a nice comfy, normal kind of tanning bed. After laying Joshua on it, I considered him. Without any water in his body, he didn't look much like the cute Joshua I had known. I knew, too, from the hatred burning brightly in his eyes earlier, he was evil to the core. How could Dominic be so good under the vampiric influence and Joshua so wicked? It must have been an inborn thing, something about their true natures. I closed the lid to the coffin, turned on the setting to high, and started the tanning process.

For an instant, I felt remorse. I'd never killed anything in my life—well, except for bloodthirsty mosquitoes and filthy flies and the like. But I would never think I would be killing a warlock, one who I had known forever, and horror of horrors, had had a crush on.

Having the demon remove all of Joshua's water from his system had been pretty wicked. But I feared worse the reprisals he would have unleashed upon us if I didn't take care of him now. Certainly, all I had to do was consider Kate's poor neck and his unbridled savagery and know I was next. Plus, I knew when he had the opportunity, he would kill Dominic without a care in the world.

I set the timer on the maximum minutes it would allow, then left the room, not wanting to be in the same room as the death machine. In the meantime, I sat in one of the manicurist's chairs and closed my eyes, nearly drifting off to sleep. But when the timer on the machine shut off, I shook the weariness from my system and hurried back into the room. Staring at the coffin, I couldn't compel my hand to lift the lid. Heartbeat thundering, I hesitated. What if he wasn't dead? What if he lunged out of the tanning bed and tried to rip my throat out?

Every strange little creak inside the building made my skin crawl. But no sound came from the tanning bed. Still, I wondered. Was he waiting, sensing me terrified, standing there, ready to pounce on me?

Gritting my teeth, I touched the lid, again unable to gather the strength to lift it. *Coward*, I chided myself. *Just do it.*

Then I reset the timer for the longest time allowed and waited.

I might be a coward, but not a dummy. Once the minutes had passed, I quickly cast a protection spell. Then before I could change my mind, I jammed up the lid, breaking two fingernails in the process, and stared into the tanning bed. All that was left of Joshua was a pile of ashes and his clothes. His parents would be stricken to learn their son had disappeared— yet if they knew what he'd become, would they be so upset?

Probably. I stifled my own upset, trying to keep in mind the monster he had become and not the cute guy I'd had a crush on for years.

I stared at the ashes, wondering how I was going to clean up the mess. Then I noticed cloths used to wipe down the bed nearby. Quickly, I shoved the ashes into a plastic sack-lined garbage can, then pulled the sack free.

Without any further waste of precious time, I headed back to the door and walked outside. After relocking the door, I tossed the garbage sack into a dumpster. But when I hurried for the car around the bend in the building, an odd aura of lights flashed in the dark, catching my eye. I immediately stopped, my heart skipped a beat, and I quit breathing.

Peeking further around the corner, I saw police lights swirling, painting the night like a disco club's flashy, colored illumination, as the patrol car parked behind my parents' vehicle.

I stood petrified, my heart beating again at a breakneck speed, my skin chilled all the way through to the bone. In a panic, I couldn't think of what to do now. I was usually pretty good at coming up with a plan. Why not now? My brain was half dead from lack of sleep.

How would I explain to my parents that I was at Kate's aunt's nail shop in the middle of the night, while Kate had a terrible neck wound, had suffered a severe blood loss, and there was a strange boy in the car?

The hair on the nape of my neck stood on end. What was I to do?

I was making sure the place was locked. That's what I would say. We worried that someone was trying to get in. Or something like that. And a wild animal had bitten Kate. I was taking her to the emergency room to get blood.

I took a step toward the car, but a hand grabbed my wrist, and another clamped over my mouth to stifle my scream. My blood rushed into my ears, and all of a sudden, my bones felt like rubber.

Then I smelled Dominic's spicy scent and at once felt his heated, hard body against me, cradling mine, his warm breath against my cheek, and I calmed. Relaxing in his arms, I asked, *"What will we do now?"*

"They're taking Kate to the hospital. She needs blood. They'll make sure she gets it." Dominic gave me another reassuring squeeze, then nuzzled his face against mine.

"But you can go places with a wave of your hand. How will I make it home in the dark with Lynetta and her minions looking for us?" I couldn't help the panic rising in my blood. We weren't safe by a long shot.

"I won't let you go anywhere by yourself. We're in this together, remember?" He tightened his hold on me as if to emphasize his point, and he truly felt like a godsend.

Still annoyed he'd tried to take her on his own when he was so weak, I haughtily reminded him, *"Yeah, but the last time you planned on eliminating her all by yourself—"*

"I changed my mind. After Joshua zapped me with that little electrical storm, I decided I wasn't so all-powerful." He wrapped his arms tightly around me and pulled me behind the dumpster. *"Were you able to get rid of Joshua properly?"*

I pointed to the trash receptacle.

He nodded. *"I've got to get you someplace safe for the rest of the night. Right now, the police are looking for a missing girl and concerned about another girl who has been badly bitten and lost a lot of blood. Kate's pretty groggy, but realized it was best to keep her mouth shut in the event you were still in the tanning salon. I, of course, quickly vanished. They might have assumed I had something to do with Kate's bites otherwise, and I figured for now it was probably best we didn't have to explain who I was anyway. Plus, I had to look out for you."*

"*Thank God for that. So now what?*" I still couldn't come up with one iota of a plan, no matter how much I wracked my brain for one. Maybe because Tall, Dark, and Handsome's touch was making me forget everything.

"*It's time for you to meet my parents,*" he said matter-of-factly.

I stared at him, the words still lingering in my mind from what Lynetta had said about him killing his family centuries earlier. I flung my arms around Dominic's neck, gave him an octopus squeeze and a long and lingering kiss.

He smiled and returned the kiss. "*I should have suggested seeing my parents sooner.*"

19

D OMINIC

TO MY RELIEF and Marissa's, my brother came to the rescue once more that night, only the stakes had considerably increased by that time. The police were combing the city for Marissa, assuming the poor girl was dead at the hands of the same beast who tore into Kate, and possibly the same one who had killed the other people in town.

James opened his mouth to speak a couple of times, but clamped it shut. Marissa slept in my arms while we sat on the bench seat of the old blue pickup, its engine grumbling as we made our way to the outskirts of the city. I was glad to be going home, if only for a brief visit. And I was even more glad Marissa was safe with me. I kissed her forehead, loving the peach fragrance that scented her hair and the way she slept against me, as if I were her savior after all, able to protect her from the evil of the world.

Then James said softly, "We have to let her parents know she's alive and well and get the police to quit searching for her. Even her friend Kate's going to be worried she has been killed."

"Remember what happened when I told you a vampire had turned me? None of you had believed it. Not until I vanished and reappeared and did some of the other stuff I could do. Then I thought Dad was going to have a heart attack and Mom a stroke. Even you looked like you were close to giving out, and you're definitely the most open-minded one in our family, besides me. Well, at least most of the time."

James shook his head, his lips curving at the corners a smidgeon. "You've got to admit when you climbed up the side of the house, it was pretty shocking."

Still annoyed I'd told the truth, had been living a horrible hell since the change, and no one had believed me, my stomach muscles tightened. "None of you would buy it. Not by the bite marks on my neck. Even now, the police and everyone else are saying it's some crazy killer. No one will consider that vampires have moved into the city. So how will we explain this? Besides, we need to wait until daybreak when Lynetta can't get to Marissa as easily. Then we can call and say we found her wandering around lost in the woods."

"No. You said you've been to the witches' and warlocks' school. How will you explain that you knew her, and then happened to find her? It's too convenient and sounds way too suspicious."

"We were searching for her?"

"Okay, listen, she called you and said something was wrong at the nail place, and when she didn't report back to you, we both went looking for her. But we have to call her parents tonight. If they allow her to stay with us, fine. If not..." James shrugged and let me conclude what I would.

I didn't like that Marissa and I would be separated if her

parents made an issue of it, but I had to agree my brother was right. Maybe it was because he was a freshman in college, or maybe not. He always did have a more psychoanalytical brain when it came to figuring the human—well, rather, *psychological* —factor out. "All right, thanks again, James, for the rescue."

"I'm just sorry I didn't keep you from getting turned by that vamp in the first place." His voice was filled with regret.

I wished he had, too. "It wasn't your fault, James. You know me, a throw-caution-to-the-wind kind of guy." I doubt if James had warned me how bad someone like Lynetta could be, I would have heeded his words. Once she controlled me with her vampire love song, it was all over. Humans just didn't have any kind of resistance to the bloodsuckers' allure.

As soon as we arrived home, every light on in the place, my parents hurried out to greet us, both looking nervously about them as if they waited for a full-fledged vampire assault. Dad was a big, heavyset guy, a football player in his college and high school days but tackling bodies in a game was one thing. He was a mouse when it came to any other kind of confrontation, and he had ulcers to prove it.

My mother was definitely a nervous Nelly. Don't know how my brother and I managed to be so unafraid of taking risks. Maybe it was our youth. Maybe our parents had been the same way in their teens. Or maybe we rebelled against being as timid as them.

When the neighbor's dog had chewed up my mother's garden shoes, it was James who took them to task for it. When telemarketers hounded us day and night, I gave them an earful. When the local Italian restaurant burned my mother's dinner— despite her insistence to the contrary—I asked the waiter to bring her a new platter of lasagna.

But they were the most concerned parents a kid could have, and for now, I knew returning home was the right thing to do.

With tears in her eyes, my mother took Marissa into the house like she was her long-lost daughter. Inwardly, I smiled. Mom didn't know yet that Marissa would be her daughter-in-law someday when we could swing it.

My father took me aside in the living area. Mom wrapped her arm around Marissa's shoulder and led her to my room to sleep for the rest of the morning.

"Son, what's this all about? James was pretty cryptic," my father said, his voice couched in concern, and I figured he'd assumed I'd gotten into further trouble—if that was possible.

My mother returned to hear what was going on in my life, and sat beside Dad on the loveseat, his hand gripping hers. I explained what had happened. My parents now knew they lived in the *Twilight Zone*, and Dad, like usual, was at a loss for words, and Mom reserved comment, her face pinched with worry.

I couldn't blame them. How many parents had to deal with a son who turned vampire? Who had picked up a witch for a soul mate? Who believed the only way he was going to get out of this with most of his real self intact was through the aid of said witch? Who had become a warlock on top of everything else?

Dad and Mom just looked shocked. I couldn't imagine what horrors they were envisioning with all the news. I wished I could reassure them everything would be all right, but how could I? I was a long way off from straightening out my life.

Dad called Marissa's parents and explained that she was at our home, safe and sound. Could she sleep here, then we would return her after Mom fed Marissa when she woke?

Thankfully, her parents agreed without any objection, a better outcome than I could have ever planned. I was damned proud of my dad. He and I had concocted a pretty good story, avoiding some of the stranger details. But being that her parents were a witch and warlock, Dad assumed they suspected there was more to the tale than we let on. Still, they promised to inform the police to call off the search and agreed to let things stand as they were for now.

The update on Kate was that she was resting comfortably at the hospital and receiving blood, which relieved me immensely. The police would be over to speak with us both later, too, so we had to get our stories straight and hope that Kate's was similar enough to ours. Though if the versions of our stories didn't match up, we could probably say she was confused from the terror she had experienced.

The rest of that morning, Marissa slept in my bed, and I wondered what she thought of my room—the walls papered in Air Force and Navy jet planes, the comforter a sky blue, and model planes strung from the ceiling or sitting on stands on every spare inch of my dresser, side tables and computer desk. My uncle was an Air Force jet pilot and it had been my dream to be one, too. Or a Navy pilot. Whichever branch of the service was willing to take me. But now...I shook my head. I imagined I might not be able to hide my unusual condition and pass the physicals.

I settled down on the tweed couch in the den, wrapping myself in the softness of a spare down comforter we normally used for overnight guests. Though in the past, both my brother and I had camped out in front of the wide-screen T.V., watching some totally cool movie that came on in the middle of the night. I would have preferred cuddling with Marissa, but despite my announcement we were soul mates, I knew my parents would haven't bought my sleeping with her as part of the deal.

Because of the exhausting night, both of us slept past eleven. Mom fixed us a breakfast spread fit for a king—with scrambled eggs, toast, sausage, cantaloupe and honeydew melon. I wasn't sure whether it was because she was so happy to see me again, or if she was trying to impress Marissa or a little of both. But we definitely appreciated her royal treatment since neither of us had dinner the night before, and poor Marissa didn't even have lunch.

Dad had already gone to work at the bank as a loan officer. James had left early to do some last-minute studying with some of his classmates for a biology test. Only Marissa and I chowed down at the table with Mom.

She studied Marissa and me like a mother sparrow watching over her chicks in the nest. Twice, Marissa caught her eye, and her cheeks flushed with embarrassment.

"I updated your parents," Mom finally said, her voice soft. It was if she hadn't lost a son, but gained a daughter, and she seemed really pleased with the notion. She'd always wanted a daughter, said they were sweeter than boys, and she would love to have one to shop with and do whatever else girls did with their mothers. I wondered then if Marissa was the kind of girl that liked to do things with her mother.

Marissa nodded at me.

I didn't think I would *ever* get used to her reading my mind.

She smiled and tackled another slice of cantaloupe.

My mother took a sip of her coffee, then set the mug down. I noticed then that we were using her expensive and very ornate Michelangelo silverware she only offered during special family holidays. Even the placemats, covered in soft hues of blueberries and a pale blue background, seemed brand new, cheerful. I saw, too, that she wore a flowery shirt and blue denim skirt, like she did when she attempted casual at a ladies' luncheon. Was she trying to dress up, but seem dressed down to make a good impression on Marissa?

I loved my mom.

Mom sighed deeply. "They seem like awfully nice folks, but I don't think they believe everything that was said last night about your disappearance and Kate's injury."

Marissa fingered a glass of milk and copied my mother's

worried sigh. "I'm...well, I'm always very upfront with my parents, though this is going to be pretty difficult to explain. Still, I don't want to lie to them."

"But what about Dominic? What if they tell the world and the police hunt him down for being one of the cold-blooded killers?" My mother's voice was filled with new worry.

If anyone knew I really was a vampire, I was certain I would suddenly be the focus of the hunt for the one guilty of the vampire-like killings.

Marissa glanced at me, then turned her attention back to my mother, and I knew instantly she was going to tell the thing I'd kept secret until now. Not that I was ashamed—well, I was ashamed about turning her without her permission. But I had felt it was up to her to tell on me, and at once, my ears burned with embarrassment. I'd not only gotten myself into this bind for good, but my lifemate as well.

"I'm one of them, too," Marissa said gently. "Only I haven't been turned as far. So it wouldn't do for my parents to say anything about Dominic's condition when I've got a similar problem."

Tears filled my mother's eyes and Marissa reached across the kitchen table. My mother took her hand and smiled weakly. Marissa said, "I do have some of the same vampiric abilities as Dominic. Luckily, I don't seem to have any need for blood."

My mother visibly swallowed but looked much relieved. "I'm so sorry, dear."

"I had to save Dominic's life."

Mom looked at me, surprise and accusation evident as her jaw dropped. "You turned Marissa?"

"By accident." I felt like a heel all over again. I explained what had happened, hoping my mother would forgive me as Marissa had.

My mother walked around the table and hugged Marissa.

"You'll always be part of our family, and I can't...can't thank you enough for saving Dominic. You're very lucky to have her, Dominic." Her tone was a bit scolding.

Nobody had to tell me that twice. "Yeah, Mom, she's really something special."

"Will the two of you be all right on your own? I...I have some laundry to do."

She always did laundry when she needed to get her emotions under control.

"We'll be fine," I said, grabbing her plate and mine. "We'll do the dishes in the meantime." I figured she wanted to leave us alone so we could discuss whatever we needed to before Marissa returned to her parents' home.

"Thank you, dear."

When Mom walked down the hall to the laundry room, Marissa poked her fork into a pile of scrambled eggs. "What did your parents think about your warlock abilities?"

"They're remarkable for adapting to ever-changing situations pretty fast. Though we really didn't discuss it much. I'm sure they'll want to know more about my new abilities—but later. What do you think your parents will say about all of this?"

Marissa wrinkled her brow. "I'm not sure, Dominic. A couple of years ago my cousin, Jack, claimed he was spirited away by a genie...female version. He left his schooling and parents behind and just vanished. Luckily, he was only seventeen and didn't have a wife or kids. But still his parents were worried sick about him. When he turned up a year later, that's the story he told."

Speechless to hear such a farfetched tale, I didn't say anything.

Marissa smiled, joined me at the sink and kissed my cheek. "We might not have believed Jack, and many still are skeptical, but he explained he had to save the genie, free her from the bottle forever. In return, he received fifty million dollars. Of course the I.R.S. is still taxing him on it, but, hey, what a windfall! Now he and his parents have this mansion on the lake."

"So did your parents believe him?"

Her blue eyes studied me, and the Caribbean color reminded me of her beautifully bewitching patron demon from the Gulf. "It's hard to say. I'm not always sure what they're thinking. But they try to keep an open mind."

I envisioned myself climbing up the side of their house to prove what we said was true.

Marissa smiled and squeezed my hand. "Now that I have got to see!" Then she gave the cutest little frown. "Hey, I wonder if I can do that?"

20

M ARISSA

MY HEART BEAT TWICE AS FAST when Dominic drove me to my parents' house in his pumpkin orange Bug. He glanced at me and smiled. "I haven't driven it since I was turned. Doesn't cost anything in gas to get around the way I do now."

"Hopefully that will all change, Dominic." With all my heart I hoped we could stop Lynetta's turning him more. But then I wondered about Joshua and how different he and Dominic were from each other. "Do you think Joshua killed anyone?"

"It's likely, the way he injured Kate. He seemed to enjoy hurting someone who was weaker than him." A glint of red appeared to flash in Dominic's dark brown eyes.

I reached over and ran my hand over his leg. Instantly, his mouth curved up.

"Distract the driver more like that, and I'll have to pull the car over and finish what you've begun."

I grinned, wishing he could. Then I leaned back against the vinyl seat. What would my parents say about all of this? I feared the worst...they would forbid me to see Dominic.

Dominic clenched his teeth, gripped the steering wheel tighter and turned to me, his expression wounded.

I felt terrible about what might happen, but I was still underage and had nowhere else to live. Witches and warlocks didn't live with human families, even if both families mutually accepted it, because of society's taboos against it. Though I highly doubted my parents would agree to such an arrangement anyway. "I'm sorry, Dominic. That's what I fear the most. They may be able to accept the story we tell them about all that has happened, but I'm not sure they'll want me to see you anymore."

"But—"

Shaking my head at him, I told him in no uncertain terms that I couldn't deal with an argument with him about it right now. I was trying to keep my hopes up but the closer we got to my home, the more I dreaded seeing my parents and the closer to tears I became. "They can ground me, force me to stay away from you, but only for a while. We're soul mates, right? We'll be together soon enough."

Dominic rubbed his smooth chin. "If they don't allow you to go with me, to stay with me, I might not be able to protect you. I can't...*won't* allow it."

I chewed on my lower lip, trying to think of a way we could still get together. He was right. We had to destroy Lynetta as a joined force, and it had to be accomplished before tomorrow evening. Then my heart sank. The witches' and warlocks' dance was tomorrow night. I would never get to go. Then again, so what? Dominic's life was at stake, and there would always be a dance next year.

Dominic kept his eyes on the road, but reached over, grasped my hand, and squeezed.

Realizing I had much more significant problems to solve, I sighed deeply.

"We can't let your parents know I can vanish and reappear in the house."

My spirits lifted, I turned to Dominic. "I'd forgotten. You can come to see me, and we can still make plans. But...what if I can't leave the house?" I slumped in my seat, feeling totally defeated. "What if they concoct a powerful ward spell over the house and lock me in? I don't know if they can do such a thing, but they might be able to. And I'm not very good at spells that I *have* learned, let alone the ones I haven't."

"We'll take it one step at a time," he reassured me with confidence and tenderness. He pulled curbside next to my house. "First, we have to tell them what has happened. After that, we play it by ear."

He took my hand and instantly boosted my courage.

When we entered the house, my parents hurried to greet us. My mother's blond hair was swept high above her head, which meant she was in one of her formal, stiff, unapproachable moods. Dad ran his hand through his long blond hair, a nervous tick, indicating he realized the situation was even more serious than they had first assumed.

He shook Dominic's hand with a firm grip as if to say he was in charge and didn't want Dominic taking advantage of his daughter.

I sighed, hoping we could get through the inquisition quickly and without too much pain.

Dominic explained everything that had happened to him prior to meeting me. I hadn't realized that being human, he'd been totally defenseless against Lynetta once she targeted him. I'd assumed he was as much at fault, desiring her kisses without any encouragement from her, as beautiful as she was.

"You're the one who is beautiful to me," Dominic said, his mind

scolding as if he couldn't tell me enough how strongly he felt about me.

I smiled.

Then I drew my serious face while my mother looked on with a stone-cold expression. Dad watched me with such intensity, I suspected he attempted to see if I lied each time I chanced to speak. When I explained how Dominic and I were soul mates, my mother couldn't contain the small gasp that issued from her throat, nor could my father hide the flinch in his neck muscles as they constricted all of a sudden. He glanced over at Dominic, who nodded.

Then the questioning began in earnest, but most of the questions centered on my claim that Dominic and I were soul mates. I thought it odd they weren't more concerned about Lynetta, or the vampires who had descended on the city, or Dominic's brush with immortality, or mine, too.

"It was written in the stars," I said rather melodramatically, waving my hands at the ceiling.

My mother opened her mouth to speak, but just as quickly clamped her lips shut.

Dad asked, "The stars?"

"*The Stars Enquirer*," Dominic said.

My mouth gaped as I stared at Dominic. We sat together on the sofa, and though we hadn't once touched, I wanted to. I craved holding his hand throughout the ordeal, and I knew he wanted to provide me solace. I needed it, but we were sure it wouldn't go over well with my parents, so maintained our rigid distance. Mom sat across from us on a wide-winged floral chair, her back stiff as a broom handle. Dad paced back and forth, but now stood still as a cat ready to pounce on a rat.

"*The Stars Enquirer*?" my mother squeaked out.

"You weren't a warlock then," my father accused, immediately jumping on the lie he figured he'd caught Dominic in.

Even I was astounded, though he sounded totally sincere. "How did you get hold of one of our magazines?" my father asked.

A miracle. If it was written in *The Stars Enquirer*, our being soul mates was irrefutable.

Dominic reached over and held my hand and warmed me through and through. He was staking his claim, despite my parents' disbelief, and his touch didn't go unnoticed. Neither of my parents said a thing, but the looks on their faces gave evidence of their displeasure. However, it was the words Dominic spoke next that drew their utmost attention.

"*The Stars Enquirer* was sitting in the front seat of my locked car the night I was bitten by Lynetta. At first, I was so concerned about what Lynetta was and how it affected me, I didn't pay much attention to the magazine. But when I returned to my home that night, I found it lying on my pillow. Still, I ignored it. After Lynetta took my blood, I'd been so lightheaded, nothing seemed clear in my mind. I thought maybe I was imagining things. No human could get their hands on one of your magazines. They're forbidden to humans, as well you know."

Dominic kissed my hand, and I felt a blush rise to my cheeks. "My father had already left for work and my brother for college before I woke from the coma-like sleep I'd been in. My mother left a note for me that she'd gone grocery shopping. I threw together a ham sandwich, then carried my plate to the table. The magazine sat at my place setting.

"I assumed then that something written inside pertained to me. In the index I found my name...in fact, I couldn't read anything else on the page, just my name. The rest of the writing looked like Greek symbols, totally foreign. Marissa's name wasn't there. Just mine. I quickly flipped to page twenty-two."

"Marissa's birthday," my mother said, her voice nearly inaudible.

"I couldn't read anything on the page except for an

announcement. '*Dominic Vorchowsky and Marissa Lakeland are destined to meet tonight, soul mates, now and forever. Nothing can break the bond they shall form. And only she can help him to win the battle he must face, while he protects her for all eternity.*' I knew it wasn't possible. Nothing can predict the future. Yet I couldn't understand how my name could be linked with a girl's in a magazine I had no ability to ever receive, nor should I have been able to read. What's written in *The Stars* always comes to pass, right? At least that's the rumor I've heard. But then again, I knew how powerful Lynetta was. Was the whole thing somehow her doing? A game she played?"

My mother squirmed in her seat, and Dad slumped down on a chair next to hers. "Soul mates," he muttered.

"I still didn't believe it," Dominic said softly. "I wasn't a warlock. I didn't know what to think. Lynetta's mind reached out to me, pulling me to rejoin her at the Hamburger Spot that night. But when I saw Marissa, I knew she was the one. At once, her blue eyes caught mine, and she held me, entranced me. I couldn't break away from her gaze, nor could she mine, until Kate yanked at her arm. Still, I couldn't just approach her and say, 'Did you know we're soul mates? You're to save me, and I'm to protect you?' She would have thought I was crazy. A witch normally doesn't have anything to do with a human." Dominic paused for a breath. "Marissa explained what happened after that."

Dad rose from his chair, then disappeared into his office. Mother just stared at Dominic.

I cleared my throat. "So you see, I have to help Dominic kill Lynetta."

My father strode back into the room, flipping through *The Stars Enquirer*. He narrowed his eyes to read the fine print, a deep frown furrowing his brow. Then he raised his blond brows and yanked at his beard. "Well, welcome our future son-in-law into the family," he exclaimed, his words a mixed bag of relief, surprise, and joy.

My mother took the magazine from him, verifying the words before she passed judgment. She looked up from the magazine. "It's written in our ancient language."

Dad rubbed her back. "All the more reason to believe, my love."

Dad hadn't called Mom that in ages. Her green eyes warmed at hearing the endearing term. "But he isn't a real warlock...from birth, I mean."

"He has been admitted in one of the most ancient ways, Sienna. He has been chosen. We always knew someone special would marry our Marissa. Very few of our kind can call a demon to their aid."

"But a human-turned-vampire?" Tears shimmered in my mother's eyes, and I joined her and gave her a hug.

"He's truly a warlock now, and if we destroy Lynetta..."

The doorbell rang and I nearly jumped out of my skin. What now?

Dad answered the door, while we looked on.

A policeman stood on our front step and peered beyond Dad at me with an almost eerily dead stare. "I need to speak to your daughter about what happened last night, and to the young man who claimed to have found her, sir."

Something about the officer bothered me. His skin was pale, as if he'd suffered blood loss. And a bandage hid a wound on his neck.

My dad said, "Come right—"

"No!" both Dominic and I shouted at once and raced to the door.

21

D OMINIC

MARISSA'S FATHER stared at us as we stopped him from inviting the policeman into their house. I could see then the realization still hadn't sunk in with her parents that vampires could exist.

"We'll speak to him on the front porch. It wouldn't be a good idea to invite him in, with Mom so ill with the flu." Marissa glanced back at her mom who immediately began to cough.

I loved her mom at once.

"I understand, Marissa," her father said, finally getting the picture. "I'll join you." He pulled the door closed behind us.

The cop stood on one foot then the other, his black, beady eyes shifting from Marissa's father to Marissa, then to me. He seemed at a loss as to what to do. I assumed his job was to get into the house. After that, it didn't matter. He could let Lynetta in anytime.

But he'd been thwarted and seemed unsure how to proceed next.

Marissa and I had the same thought at once. Both of us wiped the policeman's mind of Lynetta's instructions. Then I commanded him through telepathy: *"Return to your police station and tell them you quit. Tell your chief how much of a dog he is, and how you couldn't stomach another minute looking at the sight of his ugly face. Tell him you would rather work in a sewer for a living. Now go!"*

Marissa smiled when the man stormed toward his patrol car, a new mission in mind. Marissa's father touched her arm. "What happened? I was ready to strike him down if he showed his fangs or—"

"We used the mind wipe to clear his thoughts. But Dominic telepathically ordered him to return to work and quit his job. At least for the time being, he won't be parading around town as one of the good guys."

"Good job. The human may still be salvageable." Marissa's dad tugged at his beard again, his green eyes studying the porch. Then he shifted his focus to me. "I need to get a hold of the witches' and warlocks' council at once and alert them of this trouble. We can't have vampires turning our people. Our powers are too great and could inflict devastation on the population."

Marissa thought of Joshua and said his name softly.

Her father hugged her to his chest. "You did what you had to do. We'll tell his family. As for the two of you, you'll stay with us until we've decided on a plan. With our powers, we should be able to defeat this Lynetta and her minions."

I tentatively relaxed my stiff body. I hadn't realized how tense I was with concern over what we had to do with the policeman. And I couldn't believe our good fortune that Marissa's parents would take me in.

"Can we see Kate at the hospital?" Marissa asked, hopeful.

Her father seemed distracted as he stared off at the neighborhood and didn't respond.

"Dad? Can we drop by the hospital and see Kate?"

"Yes, yes, do that. Then return here. The council will meet at once, but I might need you and Dominic to speak briefly before the members to explain what happened to you—to convince them of the seriousness of the situation."

"Of course." She hugged her father, and he embraced her warmly. He turned to me and shook my hand again, but this time, the shake was not quite so firm, not so dominating, more of a welcome to the family.

Yet I knew not all would be well. Not in the coming hours, maybe not even in the next few days. The plague that had descended on our fair city would have to be eradicated, and all of us—humans and magic users—would have to work together to find the solution.

WHEN WE ARRIVED at Warlock Iverson's Hospital, the pungent odor of disinfectant permeated the air. Muffled voices spoke from hospital rooms, but the nurse's station was unmanned. Calls for doctors or staff blasted over loudspeakers, echoing the commands through the halls.

We quickened our pace to Kate's room.

A bag of blood dangled from a hook high above the bed, the red liquid dripping down a clear plastic tube to the body buried beneath the covers.

"Kate," Marissa said, her voice hushed, worried she would wake her friend.

We approached the bed, our tennis shoes barely making a sound against the polished floor. "Kate," Marissa said again, then touched her friend's shoulder through the thin white blanket.

The body stirred and Marissa smiled.

Suddenly, the blanket whipped away.

We both gasped when we saw Lynetta and the bloody tube tucked between her teeth as she drained the liquid, her eyes darker than a moonless night, her canines fully extended. She wore the same sexy low-cut top and high-cut miniskirt, both black as a raven's wing, that she'd worn the night she'd ensnared me at the Hamburger Spot.

She tossed the tube aside. "So good of you to come see me," she hissed through clenched teeth, her lips stained with fresh blood.

Before either of us could react, she grabbed Marissa's throat. Just a little more pressure, and she could crush her windpipe. Marissa's frightened eyes begged me to save her, but I knew if I took one step toward Lynetta, she would kill Marissa instantly. My heart hammered against my ribs and my fisted hands grew clammy with sweat.

"You know where we'll be," Lynetta said, almost with compassion. "Join us tonight, at midnight. No sooner...or she's dead." The last sentence was spoken with a savage menace.

With a wave of her hand, she vanished with Marissa in tow, and I felt like my heart had been torn out of my chest.

22

M ARISSA

COMPLETELY DISORIENTED, I tried to fathom what had happened. An elusive memory tugged at my brain. Where had I felt such a strange sensation before?

Then I had it. When I'd dreamed of Dominic's first meeting with Lynetta at the Hamburger Spot. One minute we were in the restaurant and in a blink of an eye, we were standing in the smelly alley. Lynetta had transported me?

I closed my eyes. When Lynetta had taken me to her house, cursing the fact I was a witch the whole time, I tried to clear her mind in a last feeble attempt to protect myself. Maybe because she was an ancient vampire, or maybe due to the fact she'd been turning Dominic and his vampiric blood had partially turned me, I was unable to thwart her.

I opened my eyes and found myself lying prone on a carpeted floor in a large bedroom. I'm not certain what she had done to me, but my head throbbed, and shooting pains darted about my body in a never-ending relay race. I touched my neck where the hurt originated and groaned at the tenderness. My fingers were smeared with my blood. Had she fed off me, or did she have someone else do it? I didn't remember, and I wasn't sure how long I'd been in this bedroom.

When I tried to lift myself from the floor, my stomach revolted. I sank to my knees, attempting to keep my insides from churning too much or from spilling out on the floor. Could the situation get any worse?

I took in my surroundings—one queen size bed covered in a frilly pink comforter, its canopy dressed in matching pink eyelet, a sweet kind of young girl's fantasy dream. Pink, silky drapes clung to a rod around the edge of the canopy, cloaking the bed in darkness. I imagined this was where Lynetta slept during the day, though black would be more appropriate for her wicked nature. But then again, maybe it was a guest bedroom and not her room at all.

Glancing at the lone window, the shades drawn, I could sense the day was gone. I was so groggy, every thought seemed to take forever to sink in. The day had disappeared.

Dominic! I finally recalled the vamp's last words, telling him to meet her here at midnight, no doubt for the final showdown.

My watch said it was 11:30. Would Dominic come for me now? Before it was too late? Lynetta wouldn't spare me because Dominic would never be hers if I lived.

A soft moan came from the bed. I crossed the floor and yanked open the bed curtains. Kate screamed.

"Ohmigosh, Kate," I whispered, too startled to react more than that. Then I reached for her and touched her wrist. She pulled away. I realized then that the room wasn't artificially lit, though I could see just fine. Kate couldn't make me out, but why she didn't recognize my voice was another thing. "It's just me, *Marissa*," I reassured her. "Are you okay?"

"She's going to kill us, isn't she?" Kate didn't sound scared, being her typical adventurous self, but she sounded slightly disoriented.

I must have awakened her, which could explain why at first she hadn't recognized me.

"No," I said with dark resolve in my voice. "We're going to kill her and before Dominic comes to rescue us, too, because I doubt she'll fight fair."

I left her to turn on a light switch.

"Marissa?" Kate's voice sounded scared now, like she feared I was leaving her for good.

"Getting the light." I flipped it on and four bulbs in a fan unit burned brightly. Before I could rejoin her, Kate bolted from the bed and threw her arms around me. "I thought I was dead," she sobbed.

I held her tightly, trying to give her the strength and determination I felt in my mind, though my body felt otherwise. I wondered then how much blood the vampire had taken from me. Stepping back from Kate, I studied her throat. It was still bandaged, but there were no new bites anywhere else. I sensed nobody had fed on her again. She wore her denim pants and knit shirt. I assumed she'd dressed and was waiting for her parents to come for her when Lynetta had arrived at her hospital room instead. "How strong do you feel?"

"I feel good. I tried to tell the nurse I wanted to go home, but she said my mother would come later. Instead, Lynetta arrived. I tried to clear her mind, but I couldn't." Kate reached her hand out to touch my wounds.

I grimaced, the pain still pricking my nerve endings. "I tried to do that to her, too. The fact she's an ancient vampire must be the problem." Though I felt a little wobbly, I paced across the floor, not sure what else to do.

"Are you okay?" I heard the unmistakable worry in Kate's voice.

"She's dead meat," I said, unable to curb the venom in my words. I would be strong enough to take the vamp down, if it killed me. All that mattered was that Dominic and Kate were freed.

"Can you call your patron demon?"

I stopped pacing, then shook my head. "Only once a month."

"Every thirty days, or only once each month?"

My thought processes were sluggish. I touched my neck again. "What do you mean?" I just couldn't understand what Kate was getting at.

"The new month begins a minute after midnight."

"A minute after midnight," I repeated like a parrot. "A minute after midnight! But Dominic is supposed to be here right at midnight. What if she kills us before then?" I collapsed on the bed, my strength and determination dwindling all at once.

"The lightning spell worked on Dominic. What if we tried it on her? Neither of us are as advanced in our skills as Joshua, but what if together we could fight her?"

We had to chance it. Anything we could do to stop Lynetta was worth trying.

Kate glanced at my neck. "Was she the one who bit you?" Her eyes grew big as her gaze returned to mine. "Oh, Marissa, we've got to kill her."

I wondered if I might be able to vanish like Dominic did, then quickly dismissed that notion. I hadn't fed off Lynetta, just the other way around. She wouldn't be foolish enough to give me more abilities that I might be able to use against her. Rather, she had intended to weaken me.

I grabbed Kate's hand when I realized what might have

occurred. I'm certain the terror on her face reflected my own horrified features.

"What's wrong, Marissa?" she choked out.

"I can't be certain, but she might have taken some of my witch's abilities when she bit me. She hasn't been able to control Dominic since I shared my blood with him. She was only human until now."

Kate shook her head. In a whisper she said, "She could use the lightning bolt spell on us."

"Or anything else she could conjure up that I knew how to do."

"This isn't good."

No, it wasn't good. In fact, I couldn't think of a worse thing to happen. I shivered. An ancient vampire with her own powers and now witch's abilities too. Dominic wouldn't be able to kill her alone, I didn't think. The three of us had to act together.

"Can you reach Dominic?"

I wasn't sure. My mind was so fuzzy, I wondered if that was why I hadn't sensed anything about him. Then again, maybe he was too far away. I wasn't sure how strong our telepathic abilities were for each other.

"I hear everything you are thinking, dear Marissa."

I gasped. My heart pounded with gusto and my palms grew clammy.

Kate took my hand. "What's wrong?"

"Dominic just spoke to me."

"What did he say?"

"He hears everything I'm thinking." I concentrated again, attempting to hear Dominic.

"She has fed on you and weakened you. Your attempts to sense my thoughts are draining you of energy. Keep thinking of what you and Kate can plan, and I'll continue to monitor your thoughts. I only know the spells you know and if you can't work them, I can't either. See if

Kate knows anything we can all use together to destroy Lynetta and her minions. Together, we'll defeat her. I love you, Marissa. No matter what, know that."

My heart sang with renewed hope. *The Stars* had said we shared a bond that couldn't be broken. We had to do this together, just as I had assumed. "He fears I'll wear myself out trying to read his thoughts."

"Great," Kate said. "Just like before. He leaves us to fight the battle alone."

"Not this time. The problem is he doesn't know any spells except for the ones I already knew and transferred to him during the blood exchange. I have problems with correctly conjuring up a lot of them. But once we find one that will work, all three of us will use it together to defeat her. Since Lynetta said he couldn't arrive before midnight or she would kill us, he's waiting until the right time before he joins us."

Kate sat on the bed next to me and wrapped her arm around my shoulders, encouraging the strong friendship we'd always had.

Then it occurred to me. "What if there was a spell I could never master, but you could?"

"What good would that do? If you couldn't master it, then we couldn't do it together." Kate stood up from the bed, finally realizing what I was saying. "But if you couldn't master it, neither could she."

I grinned. "Yes, Kate. What's a spell I could never master? There were several, but I can't think of anything that would be useful to us now." I hated how jumbled my thoughts were.

She folded her arms. "You never were good at turning objects to stone."

I lifted my brows. "Nor were you."

"Yeah." Kate stared at the floor for a moment. "You could never enchant a vicious animal and make them docile."

I shook my head.

"Yeah, right, neither could I." Kate ran her hand through her golden curls. Then she waved her finger at me. "You could never turn an animal into another form."

"Won't work on a witch or warlock."

"Yeah." Kate looked into space, then her face suddenly brightened. "You were never good with your Cupid's arrow spell."

"Uh-uh. It would work only on someone who was good of heart. You can't make someone evil love someone who's not. Well, actually, you can't make someone who's filled with wickedness love anyone, period."

"Hmmm, I'd forgotten that part of the spell."

I stood up from the bed, and Kate's mouth curved upward. "The berserker spell!" we both said in unison.

"Why didn't I think of that before?" Kate asked, her cheeks full of color, her voice enthusiastic and filled with hope.

"Me neither. I could never do that spell because I always said it wrong. Not that I have dyslexia, but I always transposed the key words. Even now, I can't remember how to properly cast the spell." Even though we didn't have much use for it, if a gang of humans tried to hurt a witch or warlock, we could cast the berserker spell in self-defense. The humans would then attack each other, giving the magic user time to escape.

"But we can work on it! I can get you to remember it, and then we'll nail her butt!"

Her enthusiasm bolstered me. "And her minions too."

"I don't know the spell correctly either then, Marissa. Have Kate tell it to you slowly, and repeat the words, each one in the right order for me in your mind."

I could sense the excitement in his telepathic communication. "Dominic wants us to use the spell."

Kate beamed. "Sure is cool how you guys can talk to each other like that. All right, girl, let's do it."

By the time we had finished memorizing the spell, my watch showed it was a quarter of midnight. But Lynetta had no intention of waiting for Dominic to arrive before she disposed of Kate and me.

She threw the door open, letting it bang against the wall. Both Kate and I jumped. Lynetta wore a black sequined evening gown that reached her ankles, and four-inch stilettos that I couldn't imagine fighting in. Time to party?

Chill bumps covered my arms and my heart thundered. We didn't have a choice. It was now or never, despite Dominic not being here.

Six more vampires surrounded her, all of them baring their canines, all male and wearing tuxes...a nice formal affair.

My throat grew dry. But I tried to keep my wits about me, as lightheaded as I still felt. I assumed she'd told them it was feeding time, and we were the main course on the menu. I steeled my back, trying to gather the courage I needed to face the challenge. Protecting Dominic and Kate remained at the forefront of my concerns.

At once, Kate and I began our chant, silently, in our minds. If we repeated the words out loud, the vamp could copy us and do the same to us. So we had to use the utmost caution.

"*Shelingriadan, Parcel, Evilosian, Rarificat, Michelob, Minooson, Phat!*" I heard them repeated in my mind. Dominic had copied them, word for word. Then he appeared beside me. My heart raced when I saw him, but the menace before us was still too real. We only had time for a quick squeeze of hands.

Lynetta and her bloodsuckers stood still at first, as if they'd forgotten what they'd come here to do. The three of us repeated the words again, then the berserker spell hit full force.

Lynetta vanished for an instant, then returned with a sword

in the next. With one swipe, she beheaded the tallest of the vampires, while another sank his fangs into a shorter man.

Like a madwoman and her crazed minions, the vampires tore through the house killing each other—the berserker spell had set the enemy against her own allies.

"Now what do we do?" Kate asked.

"When the last one is left, we'll have to kill him or her," I said, determined to end this now.

"Her," Dominic explained. "Lynetta is the ancient one. Unfortunately, she'll survive all the others."

A grandfather clock downstairs struck midnight with an eerie twelve bongs while we searched five bedrooms, three bathrooms, the kitchen, a den, just about everywhere, looking for any sign of Lynetta. Then we found her in a large living room filled with four couches and several chairs upholstered in black sitting beside dark mahogany tables.

Seven dead men in tattered tuxes rested at Lynetta's feet. She'd beheaded every one of them and their skin had shriveled up like white wrinkled raisins.

The place smelled musty, like an old antique shop filled with mildewed books, the home of millions of dust mites.

Lynetta had a strange look of madness in her ebony eyes while she seemed to stare straight through us at the wall behind us. Her hands still clutched the sword, blood dripping from its shiny steel blade.

"If we attempt to disarm her, she'll kill us," Dominic warned.

Lynetta looked sharply at Dominic as if she finally noticed him and took a step toward us. Was the spell already wearing off? Was she no longer under our influence to kill her own people?

She snarled. Blood dripped from her yellowed fangs. Her black hair hung tangled and matted and part of the hem of her satin gown clung to her ankles in ragged shambles. Now in bare feet, she leapt at me, swinging her sword.

"It's seconds past the hour of midnight," Kate screamed, grabbing my arm and shaking it. "Call your patron demon, Marissa! Call your patron demon!"

23

D OMINIC

I BEGAN to chant for the water demon when Marissa didn't respond. Did Lynetta now hold some power over her? As soon as the vamp leapt for Marissa, I grabbed my girl. We fell a few feet away onto one of the feather-filled couches, breaking our tumble.

I scrambled to my feet and continued the chant. Marissa quickly followed behind me, beseeching her patron demon to aid us once more.

Lynetta had barely missed us with the sword and sliced the couch instead, sending a flurry of feathers flying. Then she charged for a second time but stopped abruptly and stared at the demon that appeared before her.

"What is this?" Lynetta shrieked, slashing through the watery figure with her sword.

The water demon wavered in her liquid blue shape, showing

off her satiny curves. She laughed with the force of the rush of a waterfall, but hesitated in front of Lynetta, studying the vamp. What was she waiting for?

But Lynetta seemed transfixed at the sight of the demon also. Or was she trying to control it with her black gaze as she focused on the creature's blue eyes? She might be able to mesmerize a human, but the entity wasn't human. Could she succeed?

"Suck the water from her body," Marissa pleaded.

Her patron demon's words washed over me like a summer's silky rain. "She's the one."

"Yes, yes, please, destroy her before she destroys us," Marissa said, waving frantically at Lynetta.

The vamp still didn't react, maybe unsure as to what to do with the creature. If she couldn't slice it in two with her sword, or bite it, what could she do? Yet I was feeling panicked like Marissa and wanted the entity to work faster. But I didn't say a word, concerned if I forced the issue, the demon would turn on me. I bit my tongue.

"With pleasure." The demon's words slid over her slippery tongue, and her watery arms reached out to Lynetta as if she was welcoming a child into her loving embrace.

Breaking the spell the demon seemed to have over her, Lynetta moved backward. But the demon rushed forth like a tidal wave, and with the strength of a typhoon, wrapped herself around the vamp.

Lynetta's black snake eyes bulged. Her clothes grew wet and clung to her body. Water puddled on the floor around her feet. Then she struggled as if she suddenly realized an embrace from the water demon preceded death. Did she sense the water being pulled from every molecule in her body? Did she feel the life force being drawn from her, absorbed by the demon, leaving her cells empty and ready to collapse? Shrieking, she attempted a last struggle.

Her voice suddenly shriveled. Drained of water, her wizened body crumpled to the ground.

I stared down at the vamp. Her wet gown clung to skin hanging loose around her bones. Her eyelids were shut, thank the stars. I didn't *even* want to know what eyeballs zapped of fluid would look like.

"Thank you," Marissa said, getting nearer to the demon as if she wanted to give her a hug to show how grateful we were. To my horror, the demon smiled and slipped her arms around Marissa, soaking her to the skin.

My mouth dropped open in astonishment, but even more surprising, she released Marissa unharmed and turned to me.

Instantly, I worried that she didn't appreciate that I'd called her instead of Marissa.

After all, she wasn't my patron demon. I glanced down at Lynetta and envisioned the life being sucked out of my body in the same agonizing way. My skin chilled in the damp air.

Before I could utter a cry or word, Marissa's patron demon reached her watery arms out and hugged me, too. I felt like I'd been immersed in a warm tub while the water pressed in around me, gently and with a caressing, silky touch. "Keep her safe forever, warlock. Keep her safe."

"With every ounce of strength I possess," I promised.

Kate whispered to the demon, "Thank you."

The patron demon released me, then nodded at Kate with a small smile on her liquid blue lips. Then she whirled into a spinning circle of water and vanished.

For a moment, we stood staring at Lynetta's dehydrated body as if she still held some power over us, then I broke free of the spell and spoke first. "We have to get her to the tanning bed at once. As powerful as she is, I doubt she'll remain in this state for long."

Marissa patted her pocket. "I have the key to the nail shop

right here. Let's go." Though she tried to sound unafraid, her voice trembled.

Worried that more of Lynetta's minions might be returning from feeding any time now, I carried her body outside to my Bug at a sprint.

Marissa hurried to get the car door for me. "I thought you just popped in from the hospital or somewhere. I didn't realize you drove here."

I arched a brow. "I've been waiting right outside the house all along. I had to bring my car so I could take you girls back home after this was over."

"You were that sure it would all work out well?"

I sighed heavily. "We haven't finished tonight's work yet." I glanced at the shriveled body of Lynetta, its former beauty robbed by the embrace of the water demon. With fervor, I hoped she would be a pile of ashes before she could do any more harm to anyone.

"But you thought we would succeed," Marissa insisted.

"Working together—the three of us—I had no doubt we would make it." Yet we weren't out of danger. If Lynetta revived before we could use the tanning bed to put her to rest permanently, I feared we were all doomed.

I climbed into the backseat of the car with Lynetta, neither Kate nor Marissa wanting the job. Then Marissa drove toward the nail shop. We all hoped we wouldn't be stopped along the way, though I sensed Marissa speeding a little. How could we explain the dehydrated mummy in my arms? Witches' and warlocks' science project?

Twice we passed a police car waiting in the dark, patrolling for drunks out at the late hour. With her vampiric night vision, Marissa caught sight of them and slowed down, driving slightly under the speed limit.

Then we arrived at the nail shop. I noticed my brother's car right away, and nearby, a police car.

"Great," Marissa said, her voice hushed. "Now what do we do? If we try to carry a body into the nail shop to destroy it..."

"If my brother is here, maybe he can help us get out of this mess."

The lights in the shop turned on. James bolted out the front door with a policeman following him—our older cousin, Bill, his nearly black hair cut short, his blue eyes smiling in greeting. He and James had always been fishing buddies, so what were they here fishing for now? Bill waved at me while I sat glued to the backseat, my mind frantic as to how we were going to explain this.

Marissa parked the car, then jumped out to try to head him off from seeing Lynetta's shriveled body in the back seat with me.

"What's happening?" James asked, his voice concerned.

Marissa tried to block him from nearing the car. "We're all right, but..." She looked over at Bill who hung on her every word.

James waved a thumb at him. "He's all right."

Marissa folded her arms. *"Hmmm, if it turns out he's not to be trusted, I guess I could wipe your cousin's thoughts from his mind."*

"If James trusts Bill, he's okay. Someone needs to get the door for me, like quick. I think Lynetta is stirring," I conveyed to Marissa as Lynetta's body wiggled slightly in my arms. My heartbeat had already quickened to racer speed.

"Ohmigod." Marissa bolted for my car door and jerked it open. Kate squealed. But I hurried out of the car toward the building with the mummy dressed in an evening gown, not wanting to delay our work one more second.

"What the...?" James said, but let his words trail off and rushed after us.

Lynetta began to squirm. Her skin began to plump up. Sweat built up on my brow.

"Ohmigod," Marissa said silently. She couldn't call her patron demon again. Not for another month. We had to destroy Lynetta for good on our own.

Kate ran behind the others. "The last room!" she hollered, though Marissa seemed to already have the situation well under control, having done this the night before. She led the way.

To my surprise, Bill just followed the group, never uttering a word. I know he was used to some pretty bizarre situations, being a cop, but I didn't figure he'd seen anything this weird.

"In here!" Marissa nearly screamed.

My anxiety level grew as the wrinkles in Lynetta's skin began to fill with fluid like air pumped into an air mattress.

When she began to fight my confinement, I struggled to get her into the tanning coffin. She hissed and bared her grizzly teeth as I shoved her into the bed.

Together, the whole group of us slammed the lid down, but she thrust her hands out of the end of the tanning bed. With claw-like fingers, she grabbed the lid and tried to squirm out.

I grabbed the only weapon available. A rubber wastebasket. I pounded her head with it, trying to knock her back inside the bed. My brother tried to peel one of her wicked claws from the tanning bed lid while Kate worked on the other.

Marissa dashed to the setting on the unit and shoved it onto high, while the others held the lid shut as tightly as they could.

As soon as light emitted from the tanning bed, the creature screamed bloody murder. She pulled her arms inside the bed and shoved against the lid for several minutes. The searing of flesh burned in the air. My eyes watered while the pungent smell filled the room and curls of gray smoke rose from the ends of the bed.

James, Bill, Kate, and Marissa held the lid down. I could hear their hearts beating rapidly like mine and sweat dribbled down James's and Bill's faces while I maintained vigilance with the wastepaper basket at one end of the bed, just in case the vamp stuck her head or arms out of it again.

When the time was up, Marissa quickly set it again. "Hold the lid. Don't let it up whatever you do."

"Surely she's dead," Kate whispered. "Isn't she?"

"I'm not certain. I fried Joshua twice but assume the first time turned him to ashes. But he didn't come to like she has. Lynetta is so much stronger. I'm not sure one tanning session will do it."

Then a thump sounded in the bed and the lid began to rise. *Not dead.*

Everyone but me grabbed the lid while I readied my wastebasket weapon.

Then silence. No more smells, no more sounds, except for our heavy breathing.

When the timer had gone off a second time, Marissa set it again. Questioning her actions, I waited for an explanation.

"I have to be sure. I have to know she can't get you." Tears pricked her eyes as she fought to hold them back.

I leaned over and kissed her cheek, glad she cared so much about me. But the paleness of her skin worried me. I kept my wastepaper basket at the ready to clobber Lynetta just in case she poked her head out again, but I wanted to hold Marissa tightly instead. She seemed ready to collapse.

After frying the vamp five more times, Marissa finally consented to allowing us to open the lid, albeit reluctantly. But then she shouted, "No! Wait!" She quickly cast a protection spell, and Kate and I both repeated the chant to help increase the strength of the spell.

James and I lifted the lid while Bill held a gun at the ready. Didn't he know bullets wouldn't do a thing to a vampire?

What had James told him? Maybe Bill hadn't ever read vampire lore.

The glistening bed was empty. The room was as silent as a breezeless snowy day.

We all stared at the empty tanning bed. No ashes. No black evening gown. No dead vampire. My heart sank with defeat.

Marissa's knees buckled, but before she crumpled to the floor, I grabbed for her and lifted her in my arms.

"Lynetta took a lot of her blood," Kate said, her own voice unsteady. "Adrenaline and the will to terminate the vicious vamp were all that kept her on her feet."

"Marissa, love." We hadn't finished the job, and I knew before the night was over, Lynetta would return with a vengeance.

24

M ARISSA

WHEN I AWOKE, Dominic hovered over me. His hand caressed mine with a gentle sweep back and forth. His sensitive touch warmed me all the way through to the marrow of my bones. As soon as his dark eyes caught my gaze, he kissed my cheek. "Thank God you've finally come to. How are you feeling?"

I looked around the hospital room and down at the flimsy hospital gown I wore, and the thin white blanket that covered me to my waist. A plastic ID bracelet encircled my wrist. The awful smell of antiseptics floated on the air, but the fragrance of red and white roses stacked on the bedside table helped to disguise the odor. "What am I doing—"

"We're at the hospital. You received some blood, but..."

He glanced in the direction of one corner of the room. When I followed his gaze, my mouth dropped wide open. Dominic's brother stood holding a crossbow fitted with a round wooden stake. Like a gigantic arrow, the sharp pointed end was wicked looking. He winked at me.

"What's going on?" I whispered to Dominic.

"We didn't kill her, Marissa. Lynetta will come for us...you first, I figure. You stopped her from having me. She'll want to destroy you, without a doubt."

"We didn't kill her," I repeated, rubbing my temple, trying to recall what had happened. Then I remembered. Where her ashes and gown should have lain in the tanning bed, nothing remained. I searched Dominic's dark brown eyes for answers. "Where's Kate?"

She stepped out of the bathroom, holding a mallet and wooden stake. "Right here, Marissa." She smiled. "We're in this together."

Tears choked in my throat. I had the best friends in all the world. "What about that policeman?"

"Cousin Bill," Dominic said. "James let him in on the family secret, figuring we needed some more help. He has got hall watch."

"But his bullets won't work on the vamp. Does he know that?"

"He has been outfitted with a crossbow like James. The ward has been cleared of patients. No staff are allowed to visit, by order of the Witches' and Warlocks' Council. You have a virus that can cause you to cast dangerous spells should anyone attempt to enter the wing. However, the council met at your father's house, and they're trying to come up with solutions for destroying the evil...the evil vampires."

It was the first time I'd heard him call them by their name. I shook my head. "Great. This will get all over school by tomorrow and...the dance!"

"We'll still have time tomorrow night to attend the dance, if we can slay Lynetta before first light."

My blood heated. "If that vamp makes me miss the dance…"

Dominic kissed my cheek with tenderness. "There will be next year. The most important mission is getting rid of Lynetta."

I sighed heavily, wishing I could focus on the important issue, but I'd sorely miss dancing with the knight of my dreams. "You're right," I reluctantly conceded. I glanced down at my designer hospital gown. "I need to get changed."

Dominic pointed at the I.V. attached to my arm and the blood dripping down the line. "You are not to go anywhere, love of my life. We'll take care of her if she comes."

"Why…why was your brother at the tanning salon? I mean, I'm glad he was, but…"

"Kate's parents gave Cousin Bill permission to investigate the building after the police found her with her neck torn up in your parents' car parked out front. When Bill told James he was investigating the incident, James figured he'd better let him in on what was going on with you and me. Anyway, Bill's a great guy and is taking this mission to protect us seriously."

"Thank God they were there when we arrived, but I sure wish the tanning bed had worked on the vamp." I laid my head back against the pillow. Suddenly, I felt weary, like I'd swum the seven seas and back. So much for being Dominic's savior. I knew she'd come again for him, and I wouldn't be able to lift a hand in his defense.

I closed my eyes, and Dominic kissed my cheek again, then sat down in the vinyl chair next to me. His hand continued to stroke mine, lulling me to sleep.

"She needs to sleep," Kate whispered. "If she gets enough rest, she'll be fine."

"I can't take her to the dance if Lynetta's not dead," Dominic said with some regret in his voice.

I knew, too, if we didn't kill her before the dance, Dominic would be the vamp's forever.

~

"DID YOU WANT A CUP OF COFFEE?" I heard Bill ask James sometime later, stirring me from the sleep of the dead, though I still felt I had barely any strength.

"Yeah, another cup will do. I'll take your place at the door."

I took another deep breath, my eyes still scratchy from not getting enough sleep. The overhead light was turned off. Only the bathroom and hall lights drifted into the room like warming nightlights to chase away the nightmares. I could see anything in the dark anyway, but James and Kate had need of the light.

James shut the door behind him and sat in Bill's chair outside the room.

Dominic and Kate slept quietly in two oversized chairs. I glanced at the blood bag. Empty.

Good. I hated being chained to a metal rack in the event something bad happened. Though without a weapon, I wasn't sure I could stop the vamp if she came for me.

Time seemed to suspend. More voices drifted to me. I floated on the air, jostled about, drifting through the clouds and mist and dark, damp air.

Dominic kissed me, his eyes heavily lidded, his hands on my shoulders, his touch warm and endearing. But then he pulled away from me and sat in the chair next to the bed, leaned back, closed his eyes and seemed to fall asleep, his face at peace with the world.

I watched him for some time, glad, despite our circumstances, that he had drawn me into his world. Then I closed my eyes, too weary to do much more than sleep.

A funny burning odor wafted from behind my bed. I turned toward the bathroom and saw the vamp. My heart dropped.

Her eyes and lips hostile, Lynetta stood watching me, her face and hands burned badly from the tanning bed. She took a flying leap forward and grabbed my throat, squeezing the life from me. I tried to choke out a scream, but no one responded.

"Dominic, wake up!" *I telepathically implored him.* "Dominic, please!" *I moaned with terror and grief.* "Dominic!" *I beseeched.*

A light flickered on, and I opened my eyes. I glanced around the room, *my* room with the green comforter decorated in pink roses, the pictures of my warlock idols hanging boldly on the walls, that I suddenly realized I needed to remove now that I had my very own real one to adore. I was in my bedroom, now filled with fragrant roses. I stared at my mother standing in the doorway.

She wore her mint green robe and her blond hair hung down to her hips in sleep mode. A wrinkle marred her cheek where she'd slept on a crinkle in her pillow. "Marissa? Are you having a nightmare again, dear?"

"I...I guess so." I couldn't think. Had it all been a horribly vivid dream? I felt like my head was full of cobwebs and the memories were buried beneath them. "What happened?"

"After the hospital staff gave you blood, we brought you home."

I glanced at the windows, the curtains drawn shut. "What time is it?"

"Four in the morning. You need to sleep, honey."

"What day?"

"Friday, dear."

"The dance." I looked up at my mother's worried face. "It's tonight?"

She nodded and brushed away a strand of hair tickling my cheek.

I rubbed my temple, trying to make sense of my surroundings and what was real and what had been perceived. "Where's Dominic?"

"He's sleeping in the guestroom."

"And Kate?"

"She's home, sleeping in her own bed."

"Dad?"

"Out like the proverbial light."

Relieved, I sighed deeply. "I'm...I'm all right."

"Okay, dear. Well, if you need anything, just come and get me."

I was safe. Not only would my parents' spells protect us, but since Lynetta had never been invited in, there was no way she could get to Dominic or me.

Not long after that, I drifted off to sleep again, feeling reassured and secure.

But an hour later, I heard a noise. Something like tapping on my bedroom window. Forever, I sat staring at it. Maybe I'd only thought I heard a tapping.

Then it happened again. Like pebbles being thrown against the glass. I climbed out of bed and walked to the window. I felt much better, though still tired. My head no longer throbbed, and I was steadier on my feet. Pulling the drapes open, I looked down at the front yard.

Lynetta, still wearing her shimmering black evening gown, stood near the brass yard lamp, its pale-yellow glow casting shadows over the yard. Holding Dominic by the throat with her long, bony fingers, she gave me a sinister smile and her black eyes smoldered with hate.

My heart nearly stopped.

Dominic's eyes widened when he saw me peering out the window, and he vehemently shook his head at me. *"Stay inside where it's safe, Marissa. Don't come outside!"*

Was I still dreaming? Was I having another nightmare?

Lynetta bared her wicked canines at me. They were real. She was real and so was the threat.

Terror streaked through my system. It was a nightmare, all

right. A very *real* nightmare. I had to save Dominic. I knew Lynetta intended to lure me from the house and kill me. She couldn't get to me if I didn't come outside. But I had to try and save Dominic.

I grabbed my blue jeans and shoved my feet in them so fast I fell. For a second, I hesitated, hoping I hadn't woken my mother again since I didn't want to risk her neck, literally. If *The Stars* was correct, this was my show.

Then, hearing no response from down the hall, I hurried to yank on a sweatshirt and a pair of tennis shoes, barely taking the time to tie them.

I jerked my bedroom door open and raced down the stairs, trying not to sound like a stampeding horse.

If I'd been thinking more clearly, I would have realized I had no weapon with me. All I could think of was getting to Dominic.

I bolted outside, causing the front door to slam against the wall inside, rattling a couple of framed pictures. It didn't matter who I woke now. Nobody was stopping me. Well, except maybe Lynetta.

Close up, I could see her face and hands were a grizzled mess of fire-burned skin. Her gown appeared even more tattered than before. Like a hunter eagerly awaiting its prey, her haunting black eyes followed my every move.

I rushed forward across the lawn and tripped.

My heart leapt into my throat. *Fall on your face, why don't you, while you go to rescue the love of your life*, I chastised myself. *Really cool move.*

At once, the vamp released Dominic, who dropped to his knees, gasping for air.

Likewise, I was on my knees, cursing whatever I'd struck in the grass that had dug into my shins and would leave bruises for sure, if I lived that long.

I touched the object while Lynetta whooshed into my face, her bloodied teeth bared.

The garden stake! It was the pansy flower wooden stake I'd used to beat her with before. I grabbed the stake and thrust it upward, hoping I aimed it directly into her heart, hoping the pointed post would kill the vamp. Though it wasn't real sharp, this time I had a vampire's strength.

Lynetta screamed as the stake tore through her tattered gown. She screamed again as I drove weapon through her fragile, sunburned skin, deep into her heart. Then she turned back into the form my patron demon had left her in, her dehydrated skin stretched loosely over bones. Her body collapsed in a heap on top of me, only this time her remains began to turn to a fine gray ash.

"Marissa! Dominic!" I heard my father shout from upstairs, apparently discovering we had vanished from our rooms.

"Marissa!" Dominic called out, lifting me in his arms. He carried me into the house, kissing my wet cheeks. "You did it, my angel of mercy. You did it!"

I glanced back at the remnants of the vampire, still not believing she was really, *really* dead. But the ashes confirmed it. She couldn't come back from that.

The truth surged through me like an adrenaline rush. I did it! The witch who was average at most everything destroyed an ancient vampire as old as time. A strange euphoria cloaked me entirely in a silky sheet of bliss. I wouldn't have to strip Dominic naked and turn him over to the Council of Witches and Warlocks. I would be famous because I'd exposed the evil ones to the world. Such was my delirium when he returned me to bed.

"Famous," I muttered dreamily, and Dominic smiled before kissing my lips again.

~

"SHE HAS HAD A FEVER," I heard my mother say beyond my bedroom door. "I don't think it's a good idea."

I glanced at the window. The sun was already beginning to set. How could that be? The sun had never risen. Then I rubbed my temple, realizing I'd lost the rest of the morning and now it seemed I'd lost the day too.

I sat upright, my head spinning. "The dance!"

"Marissa?" Dominic said against my closed door.

"Yes, Dominic, come in."

He pulled the door open and hurried across my carpeted floor, his dark eyes still concerned. "Your mother says you might still be too sick to attend the dance."

"She's dead, isn't she? I mean, Lynetta?"

His lips curved upward in a sunshiny smile, while dimples dented his cheeks. "You bet." He touched my hair in a loving caress, and I imagined after having tossed and turned all night I must look a mess. "You saved me," he said.

"How…how do you feel?"

His face fell slightly, then he tried to look cheerful. "Some of the vampire traits aren't so bad."

My heart dropped. "We…we didn't stop the vampirism?"

Frowning with worry, he reached out and touched my cheek with tenderness. *"Can you telepathically hear my words?"*

My eyes misted.

"I think that's a good thing, don't you?"

I agreed. But would he continue to change, to become a full-fledged vampire—what we'd tried with all of our hearts to prevent?

He took my hand and kissed it. "I haven't changed any more since you put a stop to Lynetta's feasting on me. But I'm afraid if we want our lives back to normal, we'll have to take this a step further."

Uncomprehending, I stared at him, not liking where this might lead.

He pulled up a chair next to the bed, sat and held my hand, his dark eyes focused on mine. "We have to find who bit her first. Somewhere in our memories of her life, we'll discover who it was. Then all we have to do is locate him."

"And eliminate him." I groaned, the idea we would have to terminate another of the evil ones gave me a monumental headache. "Fine, if that's what it takes, we'll do it." Then I frowned at him in my meanest scowl and folded my arms. "Why did you go out to her?"

"I had to try and kill her. She was attempting to draw you outside. I heard her throwing pebbles at your window. There was no way I would let her entice you to leave the house, especially as weak as you were."

I poked my finger at his chest. "We were supposed to do this together, remember? She had the perfect bait to lure me. You."

Trying to pacify me, he took my hand and kissed my fingers. "I was afraid to wait too long, and I was certain you were too exhausted. So I tried shooting her with the crossbow from the front porch. Since my brother earned an archery Boy Scout merit badge when we were kids, I figured it couldn't be that difficult. But unfortunately, I missed by a mile."

"So then she grabbed you and *still* lured me outside," I said icily. I wasn't letting him get away with thinking what he had done was right.

"Yeah, good thing for my sake you came for me, too. Though I nearly died when you tripped and she lunged after you, but I was too incapacitated to make a move."

"Who tripped?" I asked, my face growing hot. Of all the stupid things, I couldn't think of anything I had done recently that had been dumber than that. Teaches people how dangerous their home environment can be and that it pays to pick up stuff and not just leave it lying around for someone like me to injure herself. "I pretended to fall on my face, to put her off guard. You know, I left that garden stake there, just in case of emergencies."

He chuckled, then leaned down and kissed my lips. "Your mother said you might not be well enough to go to the—"

"I'm going. A promise is a promise. I help you get rid of your stalker vampire. You escort me to the dance."

Grinning, he shook his head.

"So," I said, running my fingers over the palm of his hand, tracing his lifeline, "do you still have warlock abilities?"

With an incantation, he raised the bedside lamp off the table, then set it back down.

I inhaled deeply, the fragrant flowers from the hospital room scenting the air. "Good. I was afraid you might find a way to get out of the warlock dance after all."

"No, I'm afraid you're stuck with me. By the way, you never told me what zodiac sign you are."

"Libra. Diplomatic, romantic, charming, sociable, peaceable—"

Dominic laughed.

"Well, normally peaceable."

"And your bad side?"

"Don't have one."

"All zodiac signs have a bad side. You told me what I could be. So what are your foibles?"

I folded my arms, not wanting to let him know I had any more faults. "*Can be* indecisive, changeable, gullible, and easily influenced. But *can be* are the operative words. I definitely don't have any of those personality traits."

"Right," Dominic said, a grin splitting his face. He touched my hair again with a loving caress. "Okay, a deal's a deal, but I've got the real bargain." He took a deep breath. "You never asked me how well I dance."

"You just hold me close and move me slowly across the floor."

"During the slow dances, but what about the..."

"During all of the dances. One pace, close and slow."

"I'm sure going to enjoy your kind of dancing." He kissed my forehead and I sensed he was totally relieved, then he pulled a class ring out of his pocket. "I know it's not a warlock's ring, but I haven't had time to get one of those. Until then, will you wear my human's class ring?"

My heart soared that he could be so romantic, so caring. "I would wear any ring of yours, Dominic," I said, pulling it on and admiring the ruby stone that shimmered in the lamplight. Then I frowned, remembering a potential sticky problem with three witches. "What if Debbie Damint or her friends see it? They'll know you went to a human school."

"Hey, didn't you tell the girls I can cloak my abilities?"

How had he known?

"Kate told me."

I smiled. "Yeah, a warlock extraordinaire parading around as a human. Could work. But we've got to get to the dance before we're late."

He grinned at me. "One track mind. I love you, too, Marissa. Be dressed in a jiff."

THAT NIGHT, for the first time ever, I attended a witches' and warlocks' dance. If I had my way, it wouldn't be the last, but the very first of many with the warlock of my dreams. A slow waltz played overhead, while the smell of perfumes and colognes scented the air. Laughter, conversation, and music mixed together in a pleasing sound of gaiety.

Dressed in a shimmering royal purple gown with a sprinkle of glitter and pearls attached to my hair in the latest witches' fashion, and wearing strappy high-heeled sandals, I felt like a beautiful fairy princess. Especially dancing with the prince of the realm.

"The most beautiful fairy princess I've ever met under the stars." Dressed in a black tux, his shirt a sexy black, too, Dominic affectionately bit my earlobe as he moved me slowly across the dance floor.

"You know, it's kind of odd." I frowned as I pondered something strange.

"Oh?"

"They haven't played one fast dance tonight."

Dominic gave me one of his sinister smiles and kissed my cheek. "They must not know any but the slow kinds of songs."

"But it's the same band that plays for every..." I looked up to see Dominic's eyes and lips smiling. I quirked a brow. "Unless someone has influenced the human band to play only slow music."

"Disappointed?"

I laughed. "Not at all."

Then I saw Debbie Damint and her girlfriends standing against one of the walls, looking definitely like a bunch of wallflowers. *Eat your heart out,* I wanted to say. After all, if Debbie hadn't been so foolish, she could have been the one dancing with the warlock hunk.

Dominic kissed my cheek. "Never, Marissa. When will you realize you're the only one for me?"

I sighed, vowing to get over my insecurities, pronto.

"About time," he said.

We glanced at Kate when she swirled by in a pink slip of a

dress in James's arms. He looked pretty debonair, and she looked like she was in heaven. "How did he get into this affair?"

The dimples showed in Dominic's cheeks. *"He had an encounter with a witch-turned vamp—"*

I shook my head. "I don't even want to know." Though I figured Kate would fill me in later. I held Dominic tightly to my chest, never intending to share him with anyone else ever again.

"Ditto, Marissa. Soul mates forever...it's written in The Stars.*"*

ABOUT THE AUTHOR

USA Today bestselling and award-winning author **Terry Spear** has written over fifty paranormal romance novels and four medieval Highland historical romances. Her first werewolf romance, *Heart of the Wolf,* was named a 2008 *Publishers Weekly*'s Best Book of the Year, and her subsequent titles have garnered high praise and hit the *USA Today* bestseller list. A retired officer of the U.S. Army Reserves, Terry lives in Spring, Texas, where she is working on her next werewolf romance, shapeshifting jaguars, cougar shifters, vampires, hot Highlanders, and having fun with her young adult novels and playing with her grandchildren and Havanese dogs. For more information, please visit www.terryspear.com, or follow her on Twitter, @TerrySpear. She is also on Facebook at https://www.facebook.com/TerrySpearParanormalRomantics. And on Wordpress at: Terry Spear's Shifters
http://terryspear.wordpress.com/

And her Wilde & Woolley Bears, award-winning teddy bears, that have found homes all over the world: **www.celticbears.com**

ALSO BY TERRY SPEAR

Heart of the Cougar Series:

Cougar's Mate, Book 1

Call of the Cougar, Book 2

Taming the Wild Cougar, Book 3

Covert Cougar Christmas (Novella)

Double Cougar Trouble, Book 4

Cougar Undercover, Book 5

Cougar Magic, Book 6

Cougar Halloween Mischief (Novella)

Falling for the Cougar, Book 7

Catch the Cougar (A Halloween Novella)

Cougar Christmas Calamity Book 8

You Had Me at Cougar, Book 9

Saving the White Cougar, Book 10

Big Cat Magic, Book 11

Heart of the Bear Series

Loving the White Bear, Book 1

Claiming the White Bear, Book 2

***

Heart of the Grizzly Bear Series

Bear in Mind

The Highlanders Series:

Novella Prequels:

His Wild Highland #1, Vexing the Highlander #2

Winning the Highlander's Heart, The Accidental Highland Hero, Highland Rake, Taming the Wild Highlander, The Highlander, Her Highland Hero, The Viking's Highland Lass, My Highlander

Other historical romances: Lady Caroline & the Egotistical Earl, A Ghost of a Chance at Love

Heart of the Wolf Series: Heart of the Wolf, Destiny of the Wolf, To Tempt the Wolf, Legend of the White Wolf, Seduced by the Wolf, Wolf Fever, Heart of the Highland Wolf, Dreaming of the Wolf, A SEAL in Wolf's Clothing, A Howl for a Highlander, A Highland Werewolf Wedding, A SEAL Wolf Christmas, Silence of the Wolf, Hero of a Highland Wolf, A Highland Wolf Christmas, A SEAL Wolf Hunting; A Silver Wolf Christmas, A SEAL Wolf in Too Deep, Alpha Wolf Need Not Apply, Billionaire in Wolf's Clothing, Between a Rock and a Hard Place, SEAL Wolf Undercover, Dreaming of a White Wolf Christmas, Flight of the White Wolf, All's Fair in Love and Wolf, A Billionaire Wolf for Christmas, SEAL Wolf Surrender (2019), Silver Town Wolf: Home for the Holidays (2019), Wolff Brothers: You Had Me at Wolf, Night of the Billionaire Wolf, Joy to the Wolves (Red Wolf), The Wolf Wore Plaid, Jingle Bell Wolf, Best of Both Wolves, While the Wolf's Away, Christmas Wolf Surprise, Wolf Takes the Lead, Wolf on the Wild Side, Her Wolf for the Holidays (Highland Wolf, 2023)

SEAL Wolves: To Tempt the Wolf, A SEAL in Wolf's Clothing, A SEAL Wolf Christmas, A SEAL Wolf Hunting, A SEAL Wolf in Too Deep,

SEAL Wolf Undercover, SEAL Wolf Surrender (2019)

Silver Bros Wolves: Destiny of the Wolf, Wolf Fever, Dreaming of the Wolf, Silence of the Wolf, A Silver Wolf Christmas, Alpha Wolf Need Not Apply, Between a Rock and a Hard Place, All's Fair in Love and Wolf, Silver Town Wolf: Home for the Holidays

Wolff Brothers of Silver Town Wolff Brothers: You Had Me at Wolf, Jingle Bell Wolf, Wolf on the Wild Side

Arctic Wolves: Legend of the White Wolf, Dreaming of a White Wolf Christmas, Flight of the White Wolf, While the Wolf's Away

Billionaire Wolves: Billionaire in Wolf's Clothing, A Billionaire Wolf for Christmas, Night of the Billionaire Wolf, Wolf Takes the Lead

Highland Wolves: Heart of the Highland Wolf, A Howl for a Highlander, A Highland Werewolf Wedding, Hero of a Highland Wolf, A Highland Wolf Christmas, The Wolf Wore Plaid,

Red Wolf Series: Seduced by the Wolf, Joy to the Wolves (Red Wolf) Best of Both Wolves, Christmas Wolf Surprise,

Novellas: A United Shifter Force Christmas

Highland Wolves of Old: Wolf Pack (Book 1)

Heart of the Jaguar Series: Savage Hunger, Jaguar Fever, Jaguar Hunt, Jaguar Pride, A Very Jaguar Christmas, You Had Me at Jaguar

Novella: The Witch and the Jaguar

Dawn of the Jaguar

Romantic Suspense: Deadly Fortunes, In the Dead of the Night, Relative Danger, Bound by Danger

~

Vampire romances: Killing the Bloodlust, Deadly Liaisons, Huntress for Hire, Forbidden Love, Vampire Redemption, Primal Desire

Vampire Novellas: Vampiric Calling, The Siren's Lure, Seducing the Huntress

~

Other Romance: Exchanging Grooms, Marriage, Las Vegas Style

~

Science Fiction Romance: Galaxy Warrior

Teen/Young Adult/Fantasy Books

The World of Fae:

The Dark Fae, Book 1

The Deadly Fae, Book 2

The Winged Fae, Book 3

The Ancient Fae, Book 4

Dragon Fae, Book 5

Hawk Fae, Book 6

Phantom Fae, Book 7

Golden Fae, Book 8

Falcon Fae, Book 9

Woodland Fae, Book 10

Angel Fae, Book 11

The World of Elves:

The Shadow Elf

Darkland Elf

Warrior Elf

Blood Moon Series:

Kiss of the Vampire, Book 1

Bite of the Vampire, Book 2

The Vampire...In My Dreams

Demon Guardian Series:

The Trouble with Demons

Demon Trouble, Too

Demon Hunter

Non-Series for Now:

Ghostly Liaisons

The Beast Within

Courtly Masquerade

Deidre's Secret

The Magic of Inherian:

The Scepter of Salvation

The Mage of Monrovia

Emerald Isle of Mists